Tales from the Stranger's Room
Volume Three

Compiled and Edited by David Ruffle

Paperback ISBN 978-1-78705-167-6
ePub ISBN 978-1-78705-168-3
PDF ISBN 978-1-78705-169-0

Published in the UK by MX Publishing
335 Princess Park Manor, Royal Drive, London, N11 3GX
www.mxpublishing.com

Cover layout and construction by
Brian Belanger

Also by David Ruffle

Sherlock Holmes and the Lyme Regis Horror
Sherlock Holmes and the Lyme Regis Horror (expanded 2nd Edition)
Sherlock Holmes and the Lyme Regis Legacy
Holmes and Watson: End Peace
Sherlock Holmes and the Lyme Regis Trials
The Abyss (A Journey with Jack the Ripper)
A Twist of Lyme
Sherlock Holmes: The Lyme Regis Trilogy (Illustrated Omnibus Edition)
Another Twist of Lyme
A Further Twist of Lyme
Holmes and Watson: An American Adventure
The Gondolier and the Russian Countess
Holmes and Watson: An Evening in Baker Street
Sherlock Holmes and the Scarborough Affair (with Gill Stammers)

For Children
Sherlock Holmes and the Missing Snowman (illustrated by Rikey Austin)

As editor and contributor
Tales from the Stranger's Room (Vol.1)
Tales from the Stranger's Room (Vol. 2)

Welcome to Stepping Stones

We believe in providing students with a caring, fun environment where they can truly benefit from a bespoke curriculum, technologically innovative teaching and the chance to develop into confident, independent young men and women. We understand the difficulties and care about the challenges that a young person with disabilities faces. We want their time at Stepping Stones to be one where they grow both academically and socially.

The school makes provision for children who have acquired processing delays due to: acute or chronic medical conditions, hemiplegia or mild cerebral palsy; those whose mental and/or emotional health is at risk due to direct or indirect trauma; and those whose mild autism creates learning needs.

We are a small school which is entering an exciting new development phase with the opening of our new site at Undershaw, the home of Sir Arthur Conan Doyle, in September 2016. This has provided room to expand and provide state-of-the-art facilities and grounds. Together our two sites provide education from Key Stage 2 to Post 16 with both functional skills and exam curriculum pathways.

Undershaw, the home of Sherlock's creator Sir Arthur Conan Doyle between 1897 and 1907, was the location of the re-birth of the great detective following his demise at the Reichenbach Falls. Today it is the home of Stepping Stones, a special needs school, offering education to those students that fall between mainstream and full special needs provision.

Today Undershaw provides the latest facilities for a special needs school including science laboratory, music room, library, art studio, fully integrated IT and WiFi throughout the building, main hall with accessible stage and a hydrotherapy pool. The building and its amenities are available for hire and events will be run to celebrate the history and legacy of Undershaw.

The building was opened officially on the 9th September 2016, twelve years to the day from the opening of Stepping Stones as a school. The event was attended by Richard Doyle, the great-nephew of ACD who helped unveil the Blue Plaque in honour of his great-uncle.

www.steppingstonesschoolsurrey.org.uk

Here we go again…

Once more we find ourselves in the opulence of the Stranger's room on a quest for more untold tales of Holmes and Watson. Once more it is a mix of the traditional and the quirky, old and new, fiction and non-fiction. Once more we welcome one or two previously unpublished writers into the fold.

It is a collection bereft of a theme, but fortunately awash with imagination. Over-worked imagination at that. But that's not a bad thing as I hope you will agree. It is indeed a quirky mix like its predecessors, which gives voice to previously unpublished writers along with the more well-known in the Holmesian world. Voices range from the traditional Holmes to the more modern incarnations of then character, from Holmesian poetry to Holmesian puzzles. You may feel some of these pieces will not work for you, but approached in the right spirit they will.

All proceeds from the sales of this volume will go to the Stepping Stones project partly based in Undershaw, Arthur Conan

Doyle's (more about Stepping Stones overleaf) and I would like to express my thanks to all the authors who have allowed their work to help in contributing to this worthy cause.

Now, enjoy!

David Ruffle, Lyme Regis, 2017.

There can be no question as to the authorship....

David Ruffle: *David lives in the seaside town of Lyme Regis, England. He works a bit, writes a bit, drinks cider a bit and performs on stage a bit. (Bit parts obviously). He has authored eight Sherlock Holmes novellas and contributed stories to several Holmes anthologies along with excursions into contemporary comedy. He is a member of The Sherlock Holmes Society of London. Seems they take anyone these days.*

Danielle Gastineau: *Danielle lives in Southern California with her parents, her sister and two dogs. She discovered her love of all things Sherlock Holmes during the early summer of 2016 when FOX TV aired a show called Houdini and Doyle. For the rest of the summer she was reading the Canon and watching the movies, TV shows and reading anything she could find on the Great Detective and his friend Dr Watson. She has always loved to write and hopes to one day publish her own books.*

David Marcum: *plays The Game with deadly seriousness. Since 1975, he has collected literally thousands of traditional Holmes pastiches in the form of novels, short stories, radio and television episodes, movies and scripts, comics, fan-fiction, and unpublished manuscripts. In addition to numerous published Holmes essays and scripts, he is the author of The Papers of Sherlock Holmes Vol.'s I and II, Sherlock Holmes and A Quantity of Debt, Sherlock Holmes – Tangled Skeins, and the forthcoming The Papers of Solar Pons. Additionally, he is the editor of the three-volume set Sherlock Holmes in Montague Street (recasting Arthur Morrison's Martin Hewitt stories as early Holmes adventures,) the two-volume collection of Great Hiatus stories, Holmes Away From Home, the pre-1881 Sherlock*

Holmes: Before Baker Street, and the ongoing collection, *The MX Book of New Sherlock Holmes Stories.* He is a licensed Civil Engineer, living in Tennessee with his wife and son. Since 1984, he has worn a deerstalker as his regular-and-only hat from autumn-to-spring. In 2013, he and his deerstalker were finally able make a trip-of-a-lifetime Holmes Pilgrimage to England, with return pilgrimages in 2015 and 2016, where you may have spotted him. If you ever run into him and his deerstalker out and about, feel free to say hello!

Soham Bagchi *.Soham lives with his parents and a sister in a small town Siliguri in India. He is fifteen years old and is still in high school. He loves mysteries, adventures, and science and he just adores Sherlock Holmes. He aims to be a cosmologist in the future. And..........that's it.*

Robert Perret: *Robert Perret is the only known (to him) Sherlockian living in Idaho. He loves Sherlock Holmes and monsters and especially Sherlock Holmes fighting monsters and has published a few stories along those lines. He is a member of the John H. Watson Society. Like many unclubbable people he is also a librarian, where he maintains a Diogenes-like atmosphere with a draconian zeal. Shh!*

Mark Mower: *Mark is a crime writer whose passion for tales about Holmes and Watson began at the age of twelve, when he watched an early black and white film featuring the unrivalled screen pairing of Basil Rathbone and Nigel Bruce. Hastily seeking out the original stories of Sir Arthur Conan Doyle, his has been a lifelong obsession. Mark's first volume of Holmes pastiches, A Farewell to Baker Street was published by MX Publishing.*

Margaret Walsh: *Margaret was born, raised, and continues to live in the antipodes. Started writing poetry as a child and fan fiction in her teens. Interests include Sherlock Holmes, visiting London as much as she can, reading, history, and stalking* spiders with a rolled up newspaper. She has no pets (unless you include the spiders). You can find her tweeting away on Twitter at @EspineuxAlpha.

Anna Lord: *Anna had dreams of becoming a Romance writer. Unfortunately, the fictional search for the perfect soul-mate turned into a soulless hypocritical chore. Not only was she as romantic as Jack the Ripper, she had for years conducted a serial love affair with Whodunits. Watson and the Countess was the product of this liaison. No awkward sex scenes...yay! Well, not many. Anna lives in Melbourne and writes most days to stay sane and sharpen her cynicism.*

Arthur Hall: *Arthur Hall was born in Aston, Birmingham, UK, in 1944. He discovered his interest in writing during his schooldays, along with a love of fictional adventure and suspense. His first novel 'Sole Contact' was an espionage story about an ultra-secret government department known as 'Sector Three' and was followed, to date, by three sequels. Other works include three 'rediscovered' cases from the files of Sherlock Holmes, two collections of bizarre short stories and two modern adventure novels, as well as several contributions to the regular anthology, 'The MX Book of New Sherlock Holmes Stories'. His only ambition, apart from being published more widely, is to attend the premier of a film based on one of his novels, possibly at The Odeon, Leicester Square. He lives in the West Midlands, United Kingdom, where he often walks other people's dogs, with or without their permission, as he thinks up new plots.*

Geri Schear: *Geri is an international bestselling and award-winning author / short story writer. Her first novel, A Biased Judgement: The Sherlock Holmes Diaries 1897 topped Amazon's Bestselling Sherlock Holmes novels' list for months after its 2014 release. It was granted a seal by the Arthur Conan Doyle estate. Before she became an author, Geri worked in a variety of fields in several countries. Her first job was selling ice cream in Dublin's Olympia Theatre. She subsequently worked front of* house in a number of other venues, and spent four years working for the Dublin Theatre Festival. She credits her exposure to great plays for her ability to create drama in her own work. She currently lives in Kells, County Meath, Ireland where it rains a lot.

Jennifer Met: Jennifer Met's first poetry chapbook "Gallery Withheld" is forthcoming from Glass Poetry Press in 2017. She lives with her husband and children in the wilds of North Idaho panhandle, whatever that means! She often pictures herself in a deerstalker, even if in reality she has never owned one. She holds an undergraduate degree in Molecular Biology, but after working in various jobs she returned to school to earn her MA in creative writing from the University of Colorado at Boulder. A lover of nature, fry-sauce, and 90's sci-fi, she often spends her free time collecting Victorian picture buttons. She also serves as the Poetry Editor for the Indianola Review. More information, including a list of recent published poems can be found at www.jennifermet.com

S F Bennett: S F Bennett was born and raised in London, studying history at Queen Mary and Westfield College and Journalism at City University at the Postgraduate level before moving to sunny Devon in 2013. The author lectures on Arthur Conan Doyle, Sherlock Holmes and 19th century detective fiction and has had articles published in The Journal of the Sherlock Holmes Society of London. The author also owns up to treading the boards in pantos a few years back. Oh no, they didn't. Oh yes, they did! Etc...

Craig Janacek: First of all, Craig Janacek is a nom-de-plume, all his friends say so, so it must be true. He took his degree of Doctor of Medicine at Vanderbilt University and from there proceeded to Stanford for further training. After completing his studies there, he was attached (not literally...that would be hideous) to the University of California as associate professor. He is the author of over seventy medical monographs upon a *variety of obscure lesions. His battered tin dispatch-box is crammed with papers, nearly all of which are works of fiction. These have been published mostly in electronic format including The Midwinter Mysteries of Sherlock Holmes, The First of Criminals and The Assassination of Sherlock Holmes and a Watsonian novel, The Isle of Devils.*

Contents

A Difference of Opinion...David Ruffle

'It goes without saying that I freely admit you could possibly be right.'

'Possibly, Watson? Come now, have I failed to convince you as to the correctness of my deduction? My hypothesis surely covers all the points in question. I would have thought my arguments perfectly sound and my conclusion the only possible one that can be reached given the weight of evidence in its favour.'

'I believe, on this occasion at least, that your chain of reasoning is not as sound as you believe it to be. And further, your conclusion as you put it is flawed by your lack of emotion. Emotion that some would see as necessary for a full understanding of this particular problem.'

'All emotion would do is cloud the issue with tangential arguments and counter-arguments. Science surely provides the answer here, clear analytical reasoning that results in a definitive solution that none can gainsay with the obvious exception of you, my dear Watson.'

'I do not believe it renders my view any less valid, Holmes.'

'Valid only in your own mind. Not so for myself and many others.'

'I am hardly alone in my beliefs, although I speak for myself in this instance. Can belief really be measured and rejected or otherwise by science? Does chemistry or physics rule our lives so completely that is no longer any magic in the world?'

'Magic, Watson? Magic? Therein lies madness.'

'I meant magic in its wider context, Holmes. Perhaps romance would have been a better choice of word.'

'I cannot imagine any circumstance whereby romance would be a better choice of word.'

'Which leads me to observe you have no romance in that soul of yours.'

'Setting aside the notion of a soul, which we can discuss another time, I concur with and am heartily glad of my lack of romance. Does this romantic ideal of yours actually make for a better or more rewarding life?'

'Absolutely, Holmes and for millions of others who would rather live their lives that way than become cold, calculating machines.'

'Cold? Do you see me as cold, Watson?'

'In spite of ample evidence to the contrary, no I do not. You have a human side to you for I have seen it in action.'

'I am gratified to hear it my friend, but we digress from our current discussion amusing as such digressions may be. The so called evidence that you have brought to my attention is in short nothing of the kind. I am surprised you even deigned to embroil me in it.'

'But, there is the statements of reliable witnesses and remember, this is supported by photographic evidence.'

'You use the word evidence as a weapon. Such things can be faked as these obviously are. It is as clear to my trained eyes as it should be to your untrained ones.'

'I only know what I see, Holmes.'

'What you think you see or indeed what you want to see because of your unabashed romanticism. And as for these witnesses of yours, why, their statements are patently false.'

'Why on earth would they lie?'

'Why would they not? They have now acquired a certain notoriety and even fame in such quarters. You are too quick to see the good in people, Watson. It is a major failing of yours.'

'I do not see that as a failing, Holmes and I stand by my opinion in this matter.'

'Watson, Watson. How can I put it so you will understand? Let me try this; there are no such things as *fairies*!'

David Ruffle's Top Ten:

(of favourite original Sherlock Holmes stories)

1. A Scandal in Bohemia
2. The Adventure of the Blue Carbuncle
3. The Adventure of the Speckled Band
4. The Adventure of the Naval Treaty
5. The Adventure of the Dancing Men
6. Silver Blaze
7. The Adventure of the Three Garridebs
8. The Adventure of the Bruce-Partington Plans
9. The Adventure of Charles Augustus Milverton
10. The Red-Headed League

All the above are rich in atmosphere and show Holmes at his very best. Of course, ask me another day and it may be a different ten! It's not easy, this selection lark.

The Adventure of The Ten Tall Men...Arthur Hall

A RECENTLY DISCOVERED EXTRACT FROM THE REMINISCENCES OF JOHN H. WATSON, M.D., LATE OF THE INDIAN ARMY MEDICAL DEPARTMENT.

On examining my private papers, I find recorded a singular occurrence that befell Sherlock Holmes and myself during the closing days of March of 1896.

My friend and I sat before a roaring fire in our Baker Street sitting room, he in his mouse-coloured dressing gown maintaining a black mood that had possessed him for the better part of the last three days. On the table, his breakfast lay untouched.

'Do you wonder that I resort to cocaine, Watson,' he said bleakly, 'if all I have to occupy my mind are trivialities like these?'

I glanced at the pile of discarded newsprint surrounding his chair. 'You have put the most notorious criminals in London behind bars, but others will appear. You must exercise a little patience, Holmes.'

'My trifling interferences have contributed,' he agreed with a shrug, 'to making the streets of the capital safe. But what has happened now, Watson? Have we reached the end? Is crime declining to the extent where Scotland Yard can manage without my assistance? Am I on the brink of obsolescence? The notion is intolerable.'

We discussed briefly some past cases on which I had accompanied him, hoping that the recollections would lift his mood. Then Holmes became still and held up a restraining finger, inclining his head to catch the muted sounds of the early morning traffic through the closed window.

4

'A carriage has halted outside,' he said, 'and if I am not mistaken, a lady has alighted. She stands on the pavement, hesitating and wondering if she should ring our bell.'

I knew that Holmes' sharp ears would have distinguished the footsteps from those of a man. His expression lightened, and he rubbed his hands together in anticipation of a new client bringing him a problem to relieve his boredom. He disappeared quickly into his room, to emerge moments later dressed in his morning-coat. His expression was all eagerness, as he sank back into his chair.

At last came the clang of the bell, and we heard Mrs Hudson answer the door and admit our visitor. In a moment she showed in a middle-aged lady of ample proportions, wearing a rather shabby riding-coat.

We rose at once.

'Pray come and sit near the fire,' said my friend, 'for I see that the cold morning air has chilled your hands and face. Take a few moments to compose yourself. I am Sherlock Holmes, and this is my friend and associate Dr Watson, before whom you may speak as freely as you would to me.'

Mrs Hudson brought hot tea and some colour returned to our visitor's face. She looked at Holmes and myself with uncertainty.

'Place your thoughts in order as best you can,' suggested Holmes in his accustomed fashion, 'not leaving out the smallest detail. Then relate to us the sequence of events that has brought you to us. There is no need to hurry.'

'Thank you, sirs,' she said a little nervously. 'My name is Mrs Eliza Fanshawe and I reside in Kent, in the village of Tarnfields, not far from Deal.'

'I believe I have heard of it. What is amiss there that brings you straight to Baker Street, without as much as a pause to look at our London shops?'

Mrs Fanshawe gave him a curious glance. 'Mr Holmes, I have heard that your insight is remarkable, but how did you know that I came here directly?'

Holmes smiled, enjoying the mystical air he sometimes created. 'When I see from my window that your cab, by its

5

number, is one that invariably picks up fares outside Waterloo Station, and I know that the train from Deal arrived no more than fifteen minutes ago, it does not seem very remarkable to conclude that you had little time to divert from your destination.'

'That is true. I caught the early train.'

'The remains of a second-class ticket, which sticks out of the pocket of your riding-cloak, testifies as much by its colour.'

'My riding-cloak? Doubtless its appearance told you also that I am from the country before I spoke a word?'

'Indeed. It is a garment not often seen in the city.'

Her face cleared. 'I believe I did right to consult you.'

'Tell me then, how we can assist you.' Holmes was eager to begin. As for myself I had formed the opinion that Mrs Fanshawe was a woman of some perception, as well as of mature beauty.

'Let me say at once,' the lady said, 'that should my narrative prove to be too commonplace to engage your attention, I would quite understand. I have considered that the strangeness I feel about the affair might be imaginary, and that your viewpoint may be different.'

'Many of Mr Holmes's past cases were presented to us as oddities or inconsistencies,' I observed. 'Most often they were concluded in a surprising fashion.'

'Quite so,' said my friend impatiently, 'but let Mrs Fanshawe tell us her story.'

'First I must explain how I came to live in Tarnfields.' She paused, gathering her memories. 'My husband, George Fanshawe, was a sheep farmer in Australia for many years before we knew each other. We met shortly after his return to England, and married a few months later. Not long after the wedding he became ill, suffering from delusions and sometimes speaking in a strange manner.' She looked directly at me. 'You, doctor, have possibly recognised the symptoms of that strain of insanity that occasionally follows certain foreign diseases when left untreated for a prolonged period.'

I nodded, sympathetically.

'When this was diagnosed, my husband was confined to an insane asylum. He died there soon afterwards.'

Holmes and I offered our condolences, as Mrs Fanshawe wiped away tears in an effort to compose herself.

'Pray tell us, when was this?' Holmes asked softly.

'It has not yet been a year. I mention these events only because some of my neighbours in whom I have confided seem to believe that I have inherited the condition.'

'That cannot be so, surely.' Holmes retorted. 'Am I correct, Watson?'

'Perfectly. I do not know of a case anywhere that suggests it.' But it was easy to imagine how the inhabitants of a country village would shun this woman. In some such places, diseases of the mind were still looked upon with fear and superstition.

'I wanted to tell you this myself,' Mrs Fanshawe continued, 'rather than for you to hear it in Tarnfields, should you decide to help me. You cannot imagine, gentlemen, the sadness of seeing my neighbours cross the street to avoid speaking to me. Their embarrassment causes me great pain.'

'Both the doctor and I are no strangers to ignorance,' Holmes assured her, 'or foolishness. But what is it that has caused all this?'

Our visitor appeared to have conquered her distress. She drew herself up straighter in her chair, determined to tell her tale to the end.

'When my husband and I decided to make our home in Tarnfields, we searched unsuccessfully for accommodation. Eventually we rented rooms as a temporary measure, but as it turned out I am still there to this day. I live above the local ironmonger's shop. I should explain that the Old Deal Road passes the building on its way through Tarnfields, and it is there that most of the shops and local businesses are situated. Opposite my rooms stands our only tailoring establishment.'

'A larger village than I had imagined,' Holmes said thoughtfully, 'if it has its own tailor.'

'I am told that the community has grown in recent years. Since my husband's death I spend much time alone, and find myself observing the behaviour of those living and working nearby. I am frequently troubled by rheumatism, so I view life from my armchair.'

'You look down from the window overlooking the Old Deal Road?' I asked.

'Almost every day. The tailor's shop I mentioned is that of Mr Edelstein, whose clients are usually local people. Farmers are fitted for tweed suits to wear in church on Sunday, and the occasional landowner collects his morning suit. This was how the business progressed, until a succession of strange gentlemen began to arrive daily.'

Holmes raised his head like a terrier catching the scent. 'In what way were they strange?'

Mrs Fanshawe hesitated. Her eyes swept the room, taking in the gasogene, the Persian slipper full of tobacco and the jack-knife pinning Holmes's unanswered correspondence to the mantelshelf. I saw that she was still uncertain of her case.

'It was the similarity between them,' she said at last. 'At first I was struck by the appearance of a man, a little before eleven, dressed in smart morning clothes. He was very tall and stood out prominently from the locals. His top hat added to the impression of height, and both his grooming, that is, his moustache, and his bearing, made me surmise that he was an army officer, or recently had been such.'

'It sounds likely,' Holmes murmured.

'The man spent about forty minutes in Mr Edelstein's shop, before he reappeared and walked away in the direction from which he came. The incident faded from my mind, on a market day there are plenty of people to engage my interest. When darkness fell I closed the curtains.'

'The man did not reappear that day, even briefly?'

'Not at all. It was the next day, at about the same time, when I saw him again. At least, that is what I thought until I looked more closely. Something about his movements seemed different, and as he drew nearer I realised that this was another of quite similar appearance. His moustache and clothing struck me as identical to the first, and his face bore some resemblance also. His actions were the same.'

8

'Do you mean that this newcomer entered the tailor's shop, stayed for about the same time and then left in the manner of the previous day?' I asked.

'Exactly that.' Mrs Fanshawe confirmed. 'I thought this no more than coincidence, or perhaps that the two were related. Then the third man came, the following morning.'

Holmes leaned forward in his chair. 'Everything was again the same?'

'Had I watched from further away, I would have sworn so. As it was I saw yet a third man, and the next day a fourth! This ritual continued until there were ten, and then it ceased.'

'So you witnessed the end of it?'

She shook her head. 'No, Mr Holmes, but the following day passed without incident. After that the cycle began again with the return of the first man.'

'You are quite certain it was he?'

She nodded. 'His walk was distinctive.'

'Ten days, I believe you said, elapsed from the first man to the last. Does Mr Edelstein conduct his business on Sundays, then?'

'Never, the village is normally quiet on the Sabbath. The man who appeared on that day was the only customer. I noticed that the shutters were not raised, so that the shop seemed to have remained closed.'

'Excellent,' Holmes said approvingly.

He lapsed into silence then, for so long that Mrs Fanshawe became uneasy. She looked enquiringly at me and once made to speak, but saw the warning in my expression. I knew from of old that it was unwise to disturb Holmes's thoughts as he pursued a line of reasoning, especially at the start of a case as he strived to grasp the first fine threads.

'Tell me, Mrs Fanshawe,' he said at last, 'what is your own explanation for these curious events?'

'It had occurred to me that these men could be related to each other, because of their similarity. Perhaps each is related also to Mr Edelstein, since he is prepared to admit them on all days of the week.'

'On the face of it, that is a possibility,' Holmes said thoughtfully, 'but I think these waters are a little deeper than that. There are several points of interest here. For example, why are the tailor's visitors superficially alike? Why are they all tall, when among any group of men chosen at random you would find some short, some stout, and so on? Is their common resemblance intended to give the impression that they are the same man? What is the purpose of their visits, one at a time, day after day? All this seems an extraordinary way to purchase a new suit, with the shop open even on Sundays. We appear to have a most singular situation here and I am indebted to you, Mrs Fanshawe, for bringing it to my attention. I think the good doctor and myself will visit Tarnfields tomorrow, to see what may be discovered.'

'Thank you Mr Holmes, thank you both,' she exclaimed with some relief. 'At what time may I expect you?'

'You may not expect us,' Holmes replied, then explained himself. 'We shall not visit your house, nor acknowledge you should we pass in the street. It would be better not to cause further gossip. Was it not wagging tongues that upset you sufficiently to cause you to travel to London to consult me?'

Mrs Fanshawe looked full of relief and gratitude.

Holmes turned abruptly to me.

'Watson, what am I thinking of in promising your services without first consulting you? My dear fellow, you must forgive me if I sometimes forget that you have a thriving practice to consider. You cannot simply drop everything when a new case comes along.'

But he looked at me expectantly, his eyes bright. Mrs Fanshawe wore an expression that was almost pleading.

'I have nothing on hand at present,' I said lightly, 'that my locum cannot deal with in my absence.'

***

The next morning we took the early train. Holmes spoke little during the journey, sitting in such deep thought that he might have fallen asleep. For my part I enjoyed taking in the beauty of the countryside, a pleasant change to the grime of

10

London. Presently we approached our destination, and areas of moist earth began to appear frequently in farmer's fields and common land alike. I recognised the treacherous tarn that gave the village its name.

Outside the little country station we hired a trap, and were driven along uneven lanes bordered by hedgerows and trees. As Mrs Fanshawe had described, Tarnfields consisted of little more than a single long main street, with an inn at one end and a church at the other. In the distance I saw several great houses, presumably the homes of the local gentry. In another direction smoke rose from a cluster of smaller buildings, and Holmes identified these as the dwellings of tenants and labourers.

'It is not yet ten o'clock,' he said after consulting his pocket-watch. 'According to Mrs Fanshawe's account, these mysterious gentlemen make their appearance about eleven, which allows us the opportunity to see the tailor beforehand. From that good lady's description, I would say her window is that above the shops almost opposite.'

'Above the ironmonger's,' I remembered. But no one watched now.

'Quite. But look, Edelman's shop is empty. Let us see what we can learn there.'

We had hardly entered, when a small round Jew wearing a skullcap appeared from the back of the room. He seemed apprehensive at the sight of us, forcing a smile but constantly fingering the measuring tape that was draped around his neck.

'And how may Isaac Edelman serve you today, gentlemen?' he asked when he had greeted us. 'You wish me to dress you for the hunt, perhaps? Only yesterday, I received a consignment of particularly fine cloth that would look well on you both.'

Holmes shook his head. 'We are here to speak to you concerning several of your clients. Certain irregularities have come to light and if a scandal is to be avoided, with possible effects to your business, you must be frank with us and hold nothing back.'

11

The tailor's smile vanished. 'What sort of talk is this? You, sir, speak as a police official would, yet I feel that you are not of the force. Explain yourself. Who are you?'

'My name is Sherlock Holmes,' my friend answered, 'and my companion is Dr Watson. We hoped to save you the trouble of a police enquiry.'

Isaac Edelman went pale; I saw the change in him despite the meagre light of his shop. I reflected that Holmes' reputation had preceded him to this backwater of Kent.

The tailor slid his spectacles down from his forehead. He adjusted them and peered at us suspiciously.

'Yes, I have read of you. The consulting detective.'

'Then you know of my connection with Scotland Yard?'

'I do. But what can you want with a humble tailor whose clients are country folk?'

'That is not true of all of them, I think,' said Holmes. 'For example, that description would be ill-suited to the ten gentlemen of unusually similar appearance who visit you regularly.'

The tailor was silent, his eyes searching our faces.

'We have accused you of nothing,' I told him, 'but there may be grave consequences if we are forced to return to London without an explanation of these events. Suspicion has been aroused, in certain quarters.'

'I have been sworn to secrecy,' Mr Edelman said after some moments of consideration. 'However, since you represent authority I cannot see that it will do harm to speak. I am not breaking any trust, since it was also from authority that the order came.'

Holmes looked at the man with interest, inclining his head so as to miss nothing.

'Pray continue.'

'Some weeks ago I was approached by an officer of Her Majesty's Royal Rifle Corps, a Major Soames, who placed an order for ten uniforms of that regiment.'

'That will not do.' Holmes said severely. 'Regimental uniforms are made exclusively by the Depot of Military Supply. Come now, let us have the truth.'

12

'This is no lie, I swear it.' Mr Edelman would not be shaken. 'The Major explained that exceptionally, for special ceremonies, individual officers are permitted to obtain their attire privately. He told me no more than that but produced documents that indicated,' he bowed his head in reverence, 'that my work will be worn in the presence of Her Majesty.'

'When is this to be?'

'That was not disclosed to me, but I am to be paid almost twice my usual fee, with the cloth supplied.'

Holmes' expression sharpened. 'How many uniforms are still unfinished?'

'None of them are complete, as yet. The ten gentlemen have been measured, one by one, and the garments shaped. Because of their duties it has been arranged for each to attend briefly for fittings, one of which is due to be carried out,' Edelman produced a timepiece from his waistcoat pocket, 'in twenty minutes from now. Perhaps you would care to wait, if a meeting with one of my clients would dispel your misgivings.'

'I think not,' said Holmes, 'at least not at this stage of our enquiries. However, your work interests me. Would it be possible to see an unfinished uniform, for a moment?'

Mr Edelman drew himself up proudly. 'Of course. I think you will agree that I have not fallen short of the expectations of my profession.'

He called out an order and a young man appeared through the curtains, carrying exquisitely-cut garments bearing the chalk marks of a cutter's guide.

'Most impressive, you are to be congratulated.' Holmes felt the texture of the cloth and examined the stitching. 'We will leave you now,' he said when the assistant had gone, 'but I must caution you to say nothing of our visit to your client or to any other. Much may depend upon that.'

He turned abruptly and we were back in the street before the tailor could speak. We walked among villagers going about their business, with Holmes silent and thoughtful until we reached the end of the village where a tiny branch of the Farmer's and Rural Landowner's Bank occupied a converted cottage. After this and a small market area, a Norman church of local grey stone stood before trees and open fields. We retraced our steps in silence.

'At least,' Holmes said then, 'some of the mystery is cleared up.'

'I cannot see that we have shed much light on it.'

'Come, Watson. Surely the repeated cycle of visits suggests something to you? At the first, the ten men were measured. The remaining attendances were for various fittings as the garments took shape.'

'That occurred to me of course,' I looked away to avoid his searching glance, 'but I wondered why Mr Edelman gave no thought to the extraordinary resemblance between his clients.'

'You will recall Mrs Fanshawe's surmise that these men were of the military. That being so, we should not be surprised if each of them conforms to a soldier's height, bearing and grooming. Remember that beards and moustaches in particular must adhere to army regulations, and no doubt the wearing of morning dress created the impression that these were gentlemen from old service families. Edelman must have known from the start that something was amiss, but his greed got the better of his conscience. Pah!' Holmes said in disgust, 'I should have seen it all before we left Baker Street.'

'So there is nothing in it, after all. Are we returning to London then, or calling on Mrs Fanshawe to tell her of our findings?'

Holmes shook his head. 'So you believe our journey here has been fruitless? I tell you that we have not yet reached the bottom of this business. Soldiers do not have special uniforms made by civilian tailors, regardless of their rank or the occasion. Doubtlessly the local newspapers have at some time carried an account in their small print of the theft of a number of bolts of cloth from the regional quartermaster's stores. But I see there is a coffee shop just here, where we can allow ourselves some brief refreshment before observing Mr Edelman's client. The sight of him may prove enlightening.'

We were about to enter the establishment when Holmes gripped my arm tightly. He steered me to the window of the nearest shop and pointed to the display within.

14

'That ornate chair that you see, Watson, is of the period of Louis XIV, the builder of Versailles.'

Somewhat taken aback at this interruption, I gazed with some curiosity at Holmes' reflection. 'An antique shop is always interesting, but what were you diverting my attention away from?'

He glanced carefully over his shoulder. 'I saw a man coming towards us, moving in and out of sight as he threaded his way through the clusters of village folk. That he was one of those described by Mrs Fanshawe I had no doubt, since his bearing, grooming and general appearance stood out from his surroundings. His face is known to me, although I cannot bring to mind his name, so I could not discount that we could be equally recognisable to him. You see then, my dear fellow, the reason for my rather abrupt and startling gesture to ensure we remained unnoticed.'

'He is a safe distance away now, I think.'

Holmes peered down the street. 'He has turned a corner. I noticed the local police station was nearby when we paid off the trap, perhaps a visit there will provide a few answers.'

The officer at the desk was Sergeant Wills, a burly man of good country stock who ran the little station with another of his own rank and two constables.

'We read much of you in the London papers, Mr Holmes,' he declared in his booming voice. 'Also in the entertaining accounts by the good doctor, here.'

'I am glad to hear that they are of interest to you,' said I.

'Perhaps you could be of some help with our present enquiries,' Holmes said. 'We are unfamiliar with the locality.'

The Sergeant beamed. 'Anything that will assist you, sir.'

'Capital. Firstly, is there a military establishment in the area? A barracks, perhaps?'

'None that I have ever heard of.'

'Where, then, is the nearest?'

'Up at Chatham, I should think.'

Sherlock Holmes nodded thoughtfully. 'So there have been no soldiers or army exercises near the village?'

15

'Not since I was a young lad.'

'And none, to your knowledge, are planned for the near future?'

'No sir,' Sergeant Wills shook his head. 'The only real military action ever in Tarnfields was at the time of the Civil War, which we learned about at school. Some of the farms and great houses hereabouts belong to retired majors and generals and the like, though.'

'Most interesting,' Holmes conceded. 'You have been of considerable help. Thank you.'

'Is that all then, sir?' Said the sergeant, looking somewhat dismayed.

'For the present. It may be that we will meet again soon.'

In the street once more, Holmes rubbed his hands together in delight. 'Now there is one more call to make, at the office of the local newspaper. I will visit the Tarnfields and District Gazette, Watson, while you order something for us at the inn. Shortly after, we will need a trap to return us to the station.'

***

It was late afternoon when we arrived back at Baker Street, but Holmes went out again almost immediately. He had said little to me during the return journey, but I knew from his lightened mood that some of what to me were unconnected aspects of this affair, had already formed a pattern in his agile mind. I sat enjoying a pipe before dinner, wondering if he had perhaps gone to consult some military authority on the matter, when his steps thundered on the stairs. Moments later, he burst into the room.

'Watson!' he cried. 'I have it!'

I put aside my pipe eagerly. 'You have solved the problem of the ten tall men?'

'No,' he gasped in exasperation. 'The face! The face!'

'That of the man who we were at such pains to avoid, this morning?'

'Of course. Who else would I be pursuing?'

16

'I imagined that you had gone to seek advice from the military.'

A look of surprise crossed his face. 'Why would I do that, after explaining that genuine uniforms are issued only through official channels? No, the military are not involved here. I have been to Scotland Yard, but Lestrade is away.'

'I suppose there are cases he attends to without your help.'

'So it would seem. He is at present in Cardiff, investigating a series of murders reminiscent of those in Whitechapel, four years ago. However, Gregson was there.'

'Was he of any help?'

'Eventually.' Holmes frowned. 'I managed to persuade him to allow me to review the official criminal files, the so-called "Rogues Gallery". After a while I identified the man whose name had until then escaped me.'

I sat up straight in my chair. 'Bravo, Holmes! Who is he?'

'His name is Peregrine Dorrimer, a jewel thief by trade. His military career came to an untimely end in India, where he was court-martialled when his dishonesty came to light. It is known that he and his gang are responsible for a number of robberies, mostly in France and Holland, and possibly two murders. Until now they have not shown their faces in this country, which accounts for their absence from my index.'

'This man was "Major Soames"?'

'He, or one of his accomplices.'

'What would such people be doing in Tarnfields?'

Holmes shrugged. 'Gregson telegraphed the manager of that little bank. The funds held there are moderate, enough for the day-to-day needs of the villagers and local farmers. When additional cash is required, it is transported from elsewhere in the county.'

'Could a robbery have been planned then, for the next such occasion?'

'I considered this, until I discovered that arrangements are made irregularly and at short notice. No, I am convinced that the key to all this lies somewhere else in that village, which is

17

why I arranged for their local newspaper to be sent here daily. It may be some time before anything develops, so perhaps a telegram to Mrs Fanshawe will reassure her that our enquiries are continuing.'

***

Several weeks passed. I returned to my practice while Sherlock Holmes busied himself with incidents that will be remembered from my later writings as The Pirello Twins Poison Case, and The Scandalous Conduct of Mr Hector Raspindall. In spite of these, Holmes examined the Tarnfields and District Gazette on its arrival with every morning post, usually flinging the sheets to the carpet as they proved useless to him.

On a bright mid-May morning, we had scarcely finished breakfast when Mrs Hudson brought in our post. I put my own letters aside as Holmes tore open envelope after envelope with the bread-knife, his face betraying disappointment with their contents. He ignored the remaining brown paper packet, which by now was familiar to us as containing the country newspaper, until he had poured himself a fresh cup of coffee and set down the pot. Before drinking he tore away the wrapper, frowning as he scanned the columns.

'Aha!' he cried suddenly. 'At last, Watson! At last!'

'You have found something about the ten tall men?' I enquired eagerly.

'No more than five words,' he said, his face shining, 'but it is enough.'

He passed the newspaper to me.

'But this is no more than a wedding announcement, for a ceremony due to take place this coming Saturday.'

'It is to be in Tarnfields. The participants are significant, particularly the bridegroom.'

'The bride is to be Miss Sophia Pendridge,' I read, 'of St. Ives, and the bridegroom Corporal Alistair Corby-Troughton, only son of Colonel Redvers Corby-Troughton (Ret.) of Her Majesty's Royal Rifles Corps. That is surely unusual, for a marriage customarily takes place in the bride's parish.'

'Quite so. Possibly it is a long-standing family tradition to use that church. The son, of course, serves with his father's old regiment.'

'Her Majesty's Royal Rifle Corps,' I said excitedly. 'The same as the uniforms we saw in Edelman's shop.'

'Excellent, Watson,' said my friend, 'you improve constantly.'

His coffee forgotten, he stood up and left the table to rummage through the mass of files stacked across the corner shelves. Mrs Hudson had cleared away the breakfast things and I was comfortably settled in an armchair before he held up a scrap of newspaper with a cry of triumph.

'Here it is, Watson! I knew I had heard the name before.'

'That of the father, or the son?'

'The Colonel, of course. The entire case rests upon him.'

'I cannot see how.'

'It seems that the Colonel served, as a young man, in India. There he lived in married quarters with his wife and infant son until the Great Uprising, when savage tribesmen stormed the outpost. Every soul would have been murdered, had not reinforcements arrived in time.'

'A terrible experience,' I acknowledged, 'but what does it have to do with the ten tall men?'

Holmes' eyes glittered. 'When I tell you that those events had a lasting influence on the Colonel's mental state, perhaps you will begin to form the same hypothesis as myself. The savages forced an entrance and held knives to the throats of the Colonel and his wife, and unspeakable torture seemed inevitable moments before the relief column arrived. This was at the end of many months of siege, of living in the very shadow of death. Since then, and especially after his return to England, the Colonel's precautions against intruders entering his home have bordered on obsession. According to this cutting, he lives in one of the great houses near Tarnfields and the place resembles a fortress. Do you see a possible connection?'

'I confess, I do not.'

'Then imagine the predicament of thieves wishing to rob the Colonel. Finding his house impregnable, are they not likely to devise a way of approaching him or his family elsewhere, and then to use force or threats or kidnapping?'

'Of course!' I cried. 'They mean to strike at the wedding. Men from the bridegroom's regiment will be there, and so will Dorrimer and his gang, disguised as soldiers.'

'So we have surmised. The gang's first action must of course be to dispose of some of the genuine soldiers. That, I am sure, has already been arranged. However, the motive behind this still eludes me.'

'Nevertheless, I would think your theory fits the facts well enough to convince Gregson.'

Holmes sighed. 'Theories, and it is no more than that, are usually unconvincing to these hard-headed Scotland Yarders.'

'But if you tell him that Dorrimer is involved?'

'As I mentioned, Dorrimer is not notorious in this country. The best we could hope for would be that Gregson would make enquiries abroad, and by the time that was done it would be too late.'

'How should we proceed, then?'

Holmes leaned back in his chair to stare thoughtfully at the ceiling. 'Colonel Corby-Troughton, although originally from a rich family, led a frivolous life in his youth, his army career apart. For years he drank and gambled, until his inheritance was gone. Since his retirement he has struggled to keep his family on little more than an army pension, barely able to maintain his place in the community and living in a mortgaged manor house. So again we ask ourselves, what does this man possess that attracts the likes of Peregrine Dorrimer? At the moment I cannot imagine, but when I can answer that question, I will know how to proceed.'

***

Presently Holmes threw on his coat and went out before I set off for my practice. He had not returned by the late afternoon so, after telling Mrs Hudson that we would probably be dining late, I smoked a pipe of strong shag tobacco and picked up a volume of Old Sailor's Tales from the bookshelf.

After an absorbing first two chapters I looked up as the clock above the fireplace chimed the hour. The front door slammed loudly and I heard Holmes on the stairs before he rushed into the room.

'Halloa, Watson,' he called cheerfully as he took off his hat and coat. 'I hope you have kept Saturday free.'

'I can recall no engagements.'

'Capital! We shall attend a wedding in the delightful Kentish countryside.'

'In Tarnfields? You have discovered something, Holmes.'

'It is no credit to me, to have taken so long. The missing piece of the puzzle was there for the taking, at the Central Library and the newspaper archives in Fleet Street. I really should not have allowed myself to have become distracted with other matters. The affair at Tarnfields is almost concluded, save for the last act.'

'Saturday will see the finish of this, then?'

'Without a doubt. I see from your eager manner that you would like me to elaborate, but all I can think of at this moment is Mrs Hudson's chicken pie. I have eaten nothing since breakfast so ring the bell, like a good fellow. I fear that you, like Gregson, will have to restrain your curiosity until the wedding.'

***

He would say nothing more. Saturday found us walking again along the Old Deal Road in Tarnfields. Holmes had dressed in his grey tweed suit and ear-flapped travelling cap, and seemed in good humour with a spring in his step. Like a foxhound, he was impatient for the end of the chase.

'We will find Dorrimer and his gang at the church, Watson,' my friend remarked. 'They have no excuse for being late since they have been living quite close, in concealment, while their plans ripened.'

Without breaking my step, I looked at his serious face in astonishment. 'What an extraordinary statement! Either you have learned more than you have told me, or it is a guess.'

21

'I never guess,' he said. 'You know that well. How many times have I impressed upon you that to see is not enough? One must observe, if anything is to be gained.'

'Many times, I cannot deny it. What, then, have I failed to observe here?'

'Peregrine Dorrimer, in this very street.'

'At this moment?' I turned my head to look up and down the street.

'I was referring to our previous visit.'

I pondered this. 'He was attired in morning dress, the way the others of the ten were described to us. I saw him for no more than an instant, but I remember the military moustache that Mrs Fanshawe said was common to all of them.'

'Excellent. But can you recall that I have said quite often, that there are two objects of a gentleman's attire which reveal more about him than any other?'

'The knees of his trousers and his boots.'

'Watson, you surpass yourself. It was indeed Dorrimer' boots that revealed that he was living near. I saw at once that they were covered in mud of the distinctive hue that alters to a lighter colour about a mile from the centre of the village. The coating was still wet and free from marks such as a stirrup would leave, and a glance towards the inn, where passengers alight, told me that no trap or dog-cart had arrived. What else could I conclude then, but that our man walked here directly? This suggests also that the rest of the gang are not far away, since to live separately would increase the risk of discovery.'

'You astound me, Holmes,' said I, feeling not for the first time a little foolish for failing to make the same deductions. 'You always make it seem so simple. I see that the tailor's shop is closed, no doubt Mr Edelman is in attendance at the church.'

'As are most villagers in such a small community, I should think.' He noted the bolted shutters across most of the shop windows. 'Such a wedding is a major event and few would wish to miss it.' We were almost at the end of the village and the church was before us. 'Ah! We have arrived.'

The market area looked very different from our previous visit. Many stalls had been moved away or dismantled,

22

increasing the open space next to the church. As Holmes had expected, most of the local people were here in the form of a good-humoured crowd that flowed back from the church steps. Among the farmers and land-workers, others who could have been shopkeepers or clerks stood together in small groups. I noticed several clusters of soldiers in the uniform of the bridegroom's regiment, near the church.

Holmes's eyes were everywhere. His head moved slowly from left to right until the entire scene was considered. I made to speak but he silenced me with a warning gesture. 'I see that Gregson received my telegram. He has brought some good men,' he said quietly.

I saw nothing but the merriment of the crowd. By now the ceremony would be over. The faint strains of organ music died away and some little time passed. Impatience began to show in the crowd, especially among those waiting to throw flowers. Several small children began to cry, and then the church doors swung open on their great iron hinges. After an expectant moment, Corporal Alistair Corby-Troughton and his bride stepped out to ringing cheers.

At once the crowd surged forward to the foot of the steps. Ten uniformed soldiers, the guard of honour, raised their swords to form an arch over the couple.

'Now, Watson, do you see? Our ten tall men,' Holmes whispered, holding his excitement in check. 'It will not be long.'

I looked at him with curiosity, as the six bridesmaids appeared out of the darkness of the doorway and the bride and groom slowly descended. An open coach with four white horses waited at the edge of the crowd, and the coachman sat ready.

Then a landau thundered in from the street, driven furiously so that the crowd scattered. It forced its way between the coach and the steps, amid screaming women and children. Both sets of horses reared, startled by the abrupt halt.

Holmes hurried forward. He had seen, as I had, the guard of honour closing around the bride and groom like a steel trap. This was not for protection, but to force the couple into the landau that waited with its door thrown open. Corporal Corby-Troughton, confused by this unforeseen turn of events, nevertheless placed himself to shield his bride and was immediately restrained. The driver of the landau, his face concealed under the wide brim of his hat, shouted for the couple to be forced inside and held, but it was already too late. Four men strode purposefully out of the crowd to hold the heads of both sets of horses, so that neither the wedding coach nor the landau could be moved.

The men posing as the guard of honour, seeing that theirs was a hopeless situation, dissolved their formation and abandoned the bride and groom. A large party advanced upon them, led by the tall flaxen-haired figure of Inspector Gregson of Scotland Yard and the local man, Sergeant Wills.

The coachman was flung to the ground, to lie still as the gang stormed both wedding coach and landau in an attempt to force an escape through the terrified crowd and converging police officers. My doctor's instinct drove me to help the unfortunate coachman, but Holmes gripped my arm before I could move.

'Quickly, Watson, your revolver.'

I carried my old service weapon in my pocket, as Holmes had instructed me before we left Baker Street. I drew it now and stood ready, seeing that one of the gang attempted to fight his way out with his sword.

'That is Dorrimer?' I asked my friend.

'Without a doubt.'

The sabre flashed as Dorrimer, his escape cut off, flailed at anyone in his path. A stout man went down screaming and a woman was cut about the face, as two genuine soldiers leapt at him to be cruelly gashed and impaled. A child narrowly missed decapitation and the blade struck the pavement in a shower of sparks.

Holmes and I stood directly in his path.

'Halt!' I cried as he gathered himself to charge at us. 'Halt, or I fire!'

Dorrimer appeared not to have heard or noticed my pistol. He rushed at us in a mad rage, his speed unchecked and the sabre whirling. I sensed Holmes's surprise at my hesitation, but a doctor is trained to safeguard life and to preserve it, and to act otherwise is not easy. Yet strong also is the inclination to protect the innocent and to set injustice aright. I felt the instinct for self-preservation that had guided me through the Afghan War return to me. The sharp report echoed back at us, and Dorrimer fell at our feet clutching his bloodied thigh as the sword spun across the flagstones.

'Well done, Watson,' said Holmes grimly. 'He will do no more harm today.'

The police officials restrained the gang with handcuffs, while transportation to the cells in the local station was arranged. Some men of the groom's regiment were trying to restore calm to the crowd. Others, led by a portly, stern-faced man who I presumed to be Colonel Corby-Troughton, were gathered around their fallen comrades. The bride, surrounded by her entourage and a small crowd of guests and relatives, wept bitterly on her husband's shoulder.

I had made the coachman as comfortable as I could, when Inspector Gregson approached to ask me to attend to Dorrimer.

'Do what you can Doctor, please,' he asked. 'He must be fit for his appointment with the hangman.'

I saw that two local physicians had arrived and were tending to the wounded. Several times a coat or sheet was draped over a prostrate body, and heads were shaken sadly. Gregson's prediction was a foregone conclusion.

Holmes finished a conversation with Sergeant Wills, and came over to us.

'It is over. The entire gang is in custody.'

'The credit is yours, Mr Holmes,' Gregson acknowledged. 'I carried out the instructions in your telegram, and it turned out as you said it would.'

Holmes looked at the dead and injured and shook his head. 'I did not anticipate all of this, Inspector. We closed in too late. The glory, if that is what it is, is entirely yours. I shall say as much to the local news reporter who I see near the coach taking notes.' He made to walk away, but turned back to us. 'When the opportunity presents itself, you might send a constable to search the church anterooms. The ten men who formed the genuine guard of honour must be nearby, probably bound and gagged unless these butchers included them in the kill.'

'No,' Gregson smiled for the first time. 'My men discovered them, in good health. They appear to have been chloroformed, or something of the sort. One or two are sore from the ropes or stiff from the confinement, but that is all. I don't understand how you came upon this, Mr Holmes, how did you know of this gang?'

Holmes took out his watch. 'There is really not much to tell, Inspector. Watson and I must be getting back to Baker Street, and I see that there is a train within the hour. When next you find yourself near do visit us, and I will relate the whole thing while we indulge ourselves with brandy and cigars.'

So with that, Gregson was reluctantly content for the present. As for myself, I was determined that Holmes should be more forthcoming, so that I could make notes and perhaps add this affair to my collection of his exploits which may be published at some future time. I saw my chance after the trap had departed, leaving us on the platform awaiting the train.

'I rather think Mrs Fanshawe will be interested in today's events,' I said to break into Holmes' thoughts. 'Those neighbours who thought her mad will perhaps have the grace to apologise. Will you send her a telegram?'

He peered up the track, where the train would appear at any moment. 'I hardly think that will prove necessary. The lady herself told us how speedily news spreads through the village. By now she knows as much as you or I.'

'More than I, that is certain.'

My friend sighed heavily. 'I swear that you are a match for Gregson with your exhibitions of impatience, Watson. No doubt you are eager to commit this little diversion to paper, transforming it into another sensational story when in fact it required no more than the merest application of logic. Very well, we have a few minutes to wait so I will recount my findings.'

'That would be most enlightening.'

'You will recall that the Corby-Troughton house was exceptionally well protected?'

I nodded. 'A fortress, I think you said.'

'Quite. Hence I surmised that to bring force to bear upon the Colonel would be easier, elsewhere.'

'In his house or out of it, I would expect difficulties, with a man of the colonel's sort.'

'But every man has his weak spot.'

'His son, of course'

'Corporal Corby-Troughton,' Holmes agreed, 'is a fine soldier who will go far on his own merit. He refused to let his father use his influence or buy him a commission, in favour of making his own way by proving his worth. Hopefully, he will restore to their name the esteem that was lost long ago, during the riotous living of the Colonel's youth. The alliance with a wealthy and respectable family should prove helpful.'

'So you deduced the gang's intentions to abduct the bride and groom, in order to compel the Colonel to agree to their demands? But Holmes, the man is almost bankrupt. I believe you remarked upon it.'

'That much was confirmed by my researches at the Central Library. You see, Watson, I did not abandon this case while we were in Baker Street these last few weeks. I found no explanation, yet there had to be something to attract this gang. The Colonel's history held no clue, so I reasoned that our answer could lie with something acquired recently. Also, I kept in mind that Dorrimer's activities had until now been confined to France and Holland, and suspected some sort of connection.'

'It was to look for a recent change in the family fortunes then, that you visited Fleet Street?' I ventured.

'Indeed. That place is to events of late, what history books are to the past. Nowhere else is such an accumulation of facts from here and abroad to be found so easily. I have a slight acquaintance with the editor of one of the great dailies, who was good enough to allow me an hour in the archives.'

'But the sheer bulk of information must have been enormous. How did you find the items you searched for?'

'I had a fair idea of the nature of the articles that were relevant. Any connection with the Corby-Troughton family and their known friends and associates was the starting point, then a link with the Continent.'

'Which you found, no doubt?'

Holmes stared into the distance, where a plume of smoke had appeared and was moving slowly up the gradient. 'I scoured every issue of four periodicals for the past ten months. My first discovery was of the death by natural causes of Hans van Droken, in Amsterdam.'

'Ah, the diamond king.'

'The same. You will recall that, after spending most of his life in the South African diamond fields, he retired with his considerable fortune to his native Holland, it must be eight or nine years ago. When I read the account of his death, I knew I had found my link.'

'I see. That country was one where Dorrimer and his gang operated.'

'More to the point, a footnote mentioned a distant cousin of van Droken, living in England.'

Suddenly the reason behind this whole affair became clear to me. 'Colonel Redvers Corby-Troughton!'

'I never get your measure, Watson.' Holmes' hawk-like features broke into a smile. 'There is no way to know whether the gang had plans to rob van Droken, but in any case he died before they could strike. In accordance with his will the estate was split between a number of beneficiaries, with a single bequest to the English cousin.'

'Which is what the gang were after, the Colonel's inheritance.' I said excitedly.

'Precisely. They were prepared to go to any lengths to lay their hands on it. It seems that van Droken was repaying an old debt, possibly the Colonel had helped to finance his early prospecting expeditions. The bequest was a handsome one, which could indeed transform the Corby-Troughton's fortunes. It was the Moon of Transvaal.'

'One of the most precious gems ever discovered,' I retorted.

'And so the reason behind the masquerade and the entire sequence of events becomes clear,' Holmes said as the train pulled into the little station. 'This has, I fear, been an uninspiring case, although it presented one or two unique features. Now that

I have done my best to   satisfy your curiosity, let us return with all speed to London. I am glad to say that things seem to be improving there, since I have two appointments in Baker Street this evening. I trust that either or both of these will provide a more stimulating challenge.'

Arthur Hall's Top Ten:

1. The Hound of the Baskervilles
2. The Adventure of the Speckled Band
3. The Red-Headed League
4. The Adventure of the Musgrave Ritual
5. The Sign of Four
6. The Adventure of the Greek Interpreter
7. The Adventure of the Copper Beeches
8. The Adventure of the Engineers's Thumb
9. The Adventure of the Resident Patient
10. The Adventure of the Devil's Foot

'What is it, Holmes?'

'It's a hat, Watson.'

Sorting out the Suspects...set by Mark Mower

Ten anagrams of characters from the world of Holmes and Watson for you to identify. No titles are included (e.g. Colonel), but the stories in which they appear are shown in brackets:

1. End earlier (*A Scandal in Bohemia*)

2. We do lack joy (*The Adventure of the Solitary Cyclist*)

3. My major satire (*The Final Problem*)

4. Great blunderer (*The Illustrious Client*)

5. Army man sort (*The Sign of the Four*)

6. Hit volunteer (*The Copper Beeches*)

7. Clap every entry (*The Resident Patient*)

8. Shelter none (*The Speckled Band*)

9. Chivalry thereto (*The Engineer's Thumb*)

10. Arranged in bath (*The Three Garridebs*)

Mark Mower's Top Ten:

1. The Hound of the Baskervilles
2. A Scandal in Bohemia
3. The Adventure of the Dancing Men
4. The Adventure of the Creeping Man
5. The Red-Headed League
6. A Study in Scarlet
7. The Adventure of the Blue Carbuncle
8. The Adventure of the Speckled Band
9. Silver Blaze
10. The Adventure of the Solitary Cyclist

Baffles…Anna Lord

One hot and steamy Singapore night, the thief dubbed 'Baffles' stole a teapot from a hotel situated on Beach Road. It was not just any teapot. It was not just any hotel. And on the case was not just any detective.

It was Colonel Bulwer Cumberbutch, a man distantly related to Sir Stanford Raffles (no relation to Stamford for whom the esteemed establishment was named); a man tall, gaunt, abstemious, in his forties, shrewd, sharp, and immensely egotistical.

The owner of the teapot was Madame Fang, a descendant of the Manchu clan, and a close personal friend of the Empress Dowager Cixi. In a rare and reckless moment of weakness, Madame Fang had been persuaded to loan her priceless teapot to the Chinese Teapot Exhibition organised by Raffles Hotel to celebrate the success of their Tiffin Tearoom, under the auspices of Miss Luxi Gong, curator of exquisite oriental artefacts of sublime provenance.

Madame Fang had been swayed by the fact her loathsome ex-lover, Mr Zhou Zang, was loaning five teapots from his own personal collection to the exhibition. His idiosyncratic collectibles, although charming, ornamental, original and valuable, were not a patch on her incomparable gem.

Into this imbroglio stepped Mr Sherlock Holmes and Dr John Watson. They had been invited by the Sarkies Brothers to solve the case of the Giant Rat of Singapore, a species related to the Giant Rat of Sumatra. The mysterious creature had been terrorising staff and guests at Number One Beach Road from the time the Palm Court had been added, and it was high-time to put a stop to it…

"I say, did you see who leapt out of that rickshaw just ahead of us?" I fanned my face with my Panama hat as the shirtless rickshaw boy, reeking of spicy sambal sauce and opium sweat, gasped for breath.

Sherlock was scraping flecks of red laterite mud off the rickshaw wheels to add to his collection. "Are you referring to the Cantonese lady clutching the Pekinese dog?"

"How do you know she's Cantonese?"

"I heard her address her rickshaw wallah."

"She barely spoke three words to him," I protested, watching as he gave a large handful of *kepengs* to the rickshaw boy.

"Nevertheless, she employed the Yue dialect which lacks tonal distinctions in the initial and medial consonants."

"I think that rickshaw boy just got the better of you," I remarked with asperity. "I noticed he went around the block instead of taking the shortest route to the hotel."

"Of course he did. He would rather run an extra mile into an evil headwind than pass the mortuary. It is full of hungry ghosts and he doesn't want to pick one up. What was it you were you saying about the rickshaw ahead of us?"

"Oh, that - not the Cantonese lady," I muttered absently, distracted by the cicadas shrilling in the forecourt. "I meant the other rickshaw?"

"The one carrying the oriental Hokkien gentleman?"

"Hokkien?" I challenged, taking my friend to task, feeling fractious in the merciless tropical heat. I was starting to believe he was making things up to annoy me. He scavenged something small and shiny lying near a shredded banana leaf before straightening up to study it more closely. He picked up a bit of green stuff too. I despaired my friend was becoming a connoisseur of the world's detritus! "The oriental gentleman didn't speak one word to the rickshaw wallah, so you couldn't possibly deduct he was Hokkien."

"When the gentleman alighted from the rickshaw he turned to face the street with the Buddhist temple that houses the Princess of Heaven, a goddess worshipped by the Fujian who

35

favour the *lingua franca* of Singapore: Hokkien. I saw him bow his head reverently ever so slightly in said direction."

"Oh, well, not him either." Damned cicadas! "I meant the other chap – Colonel Bulwer Cumberbutch. I met him once when I was serving with the Fifth Northumberland Fusiliers in Bombay. I heard from a chap at my club that he had set himself up as a consulting detective in the Far East. Word has it that he has made quite a name for himself."

The way Sherlock's left brow shot north indicated I finally knew something he didn't! Feeling chuffed, I said, "I could murder a G&T in the famous Raffles bar."

Sherlock, looking pensive, paused momentarily at the colonial threshold like a bride sans groom. "Do you notice something missing, Watson?"

"Our luggage," said I with a jocular inflection, heartened by the promise of a G&T. "I hope it hasn't gone by way of Borneo or Batavia!"

He failed to crack a smile. I despaired at his lack of pawky humour and put it down to the fact he sensed a rival on the scene. Colonel Cumberbutch even looked like Sherlock. If it were not for Bulwer's ginger beard they would have passed for twins.

Electric fans circulated cool air through the triple height foyer, and I must say it beat a Bengali *punkah* puller with a bit of string attached to one toe and the other end attached to a frayed scrap of swaying curtain.

I was looking for the shortest route to the bar when we were accosted by the manager of the hotel, Mr Soolem, who gesticulated like an orang-utan on heat. With some force, he directed us toward the Tiffin Tearoom. I baulked at the prospect of a hot cuppa, but Sherlock, who spoke fluent gibberish on top of Cantonese and Hokkien, allowed himself to be led by the nose.

It didn't take Sherlock long to ascertain Colonel Cumberbutch had returned to Singapore that very morning from Australia, where he had solved the case of the phantom jumbuck, and had immediately been summoned to Raffles Hotel. I was somewhat relieved to discover he hadn't been called in on the case of the Giant Rat of Singapore as well. Introductions were conducted and then we listened in earnest to the details of the robbery.

A Yixing teapot had been stolen during the night. It was part of an exhibit organised by Miss Luxi Gong, an attractive Singaporean-Chinese native, to celebrate the success of the Tiffin Tearoom.

I failed to muster concern. Really, these colonial chaps must be suffering from heat stroke and too much curry in their *laksa*. How valuable could a teapot be? I soon found out. The teapot was priceless. Moulded from purple sand/clay, shaped by hand by a holy monk from the Jinsha Temple during the Ming Dynasty, it belonged to Madame Fang, the po-faced Cantonese lady with the scrunch-faced Pekinese on her lap, sitting in the far corner and listening intently to every word.

In the opposite corner sat the Hokkien gentleman. His name was Mr Zang Zhou. He had five valuable teapots in the exhibit; none had been stolen. He had hurried to the scene of the crime nonetheless. By the look on his face, he had come to gloat.

Between the yin and the yang - like a Chinese wall of silence - stood Dr Hu, a tiny wizened fellow with a shaved head and a long pigtail, a Feng Shui geomancer, summoned by the Sarkies Brothers to check for poison arrows. Not real arrows, mind, but invisible ones that are much more dangerous and likely to give the culprit the heebie-jeebies until he confesses.

My tongue was hanging out for that G&T but I could see Sherlock was riveted. Mr Soolem continued to gibber and gesticulate. I quenched my thirst on a platter of jackfruit with a squeeze of fresh lime.

Miss Luxi Gong had disappeared during the night. Things were not looking good for the attractive teapot curator. I thought the case would soon be solved if they checked Rochor Wharf, Johnson's Pier or Sailor Town.

The hotel doorman, a fierce Sikh with a marmoset permanently perched on his broad shoulder, had also disappeared. The marmoset was also missing. Clearly, Sherlock was on top of his game; he had an uncanny sense for the dastardly. Things were looking cut and dried. The Sikh had assisted the cute curator and the two of them had fled into the tropical twilight. The doorman had probably hidden the teapot under his turban. A search of flophouses and sampans would not go amiss. A teapot might be easy to hide but a marmoset not so much.

Attention turned to the vitrine that had housed the purloined teapot. It was a pastiche of colonial-oriental design: glass case on Queen Anne legs with a pagoda style roof. Inside was a large green python with a large lump about halfway down its sinuous body. It suddenly occurred to me the python may have decided to have some tea with his tiffin. This case was getting easier and easier. I helped myself to some diced pineapple skewered on little bamboo sticks.

The only other thing of note was the horrible scream during the night. Every guest at the hotel had heard it. It sounded as if all the demons of hell had been let loose to party. Half the guests had immediately checked out and transferred to the slightly less fashionable but much cheaper Hotel Europa. The other half were being attended to by the Sarkies Brothers' personal physician.

One last thing. The thief had let slip his signature tool of trade – a black cat-burglar mask - inside the glass vitrine as he made a grab for the teapot. That's how everyone knew it was the work of the inimitable Baffles. I might add at this point, that although a python does not use venom to kill, it does have long sharp fangs for gripping prey, hence, not a good idea to go waving your hand about inside his glass pagoda more than once.

Sherlock extracted his magnifying glass and got down on all fours in the meticulous search for clues. Bulwer Cumberbutch did likewise. I stole a glance at the lumpy green python coiling up with indigestion inside the vitrine and lighted my pipe while I took a stroll to the wall of windows where tall palms swayed in the courtyard and a miniature banyan tree grew in a red pot, bonsai style. Tomorrow I fancied sampling some Malay curry served on a banana leaf from a street hawker and catching that lecture by the National Geographic Society on Borneo head-hunters. I tried picturing Sherlock with a shrunken head.

Sherlock found four hairs: One bristly red hair, one fine black hair, one black hair with a greenish tinge, and one short black hair with some white on the tip that had a distinctive on-the-nose smell. He looked incredibly pleased with himself, some might say conceited, but not me.

Bulwer Cumberbutch found some grey pebbles that had a truly noxious odour. "Slowly, slowly, catchy monkey," he said smugly, rolling the pebbles in the palm of his hand like a gambler rolling a lucky dice.

The Sarkies Brothers arrived, and the twin detectives stepped forward to outline their theories. Colonel Cumberbutch went first, and I admit I was annoyed when he said the thief wanted everyone to think the teapot was inside the python. The python had in fact been fed a juicy rat so that the thief could make good the grab. Miss Luxi Gong and the Sikh doorman would be found quayside, waiting to board one of the ships due to pull anchor at midnight. He named several cargo vessels heading for the Bay of Bengal. The pebbles were in fact bits of gravel from Outram Road which was being graded by coolies, and which the Sikh traversed on his way to work each morning. They had stuck to the underside of his boots; proof that he had entered the Tiffin Tearoom in the night to assist Miss Gong to purloin the Yixing. The black cat-burglar mask was dropped deliberately to make everyone think the burglar was Baffles. The marmoset gave a shriek of joy that echoed to the rafters as the pair made good their escape. Case closed. The smug smile stretched to a triumphant grin when Mr Soolem lost his head and applauded.

Sherlock gave a dry cough to clear his throat. I feared a long explanation and longed for that G&T. My friend had finally met his match.

"Inside the *morelia viridus*," said he, never one to concede defeat or choose not to show-off, "the green python," he elaborated for those who were not au fait with snake taxonomy, "you will find neither a rat nor the teapot, but the marmoset. I have a fine hair here which belongs to the primate family, specifically, *callithrix jacchus*; the common marmoset." He held it up for all to see; or not. "And I have observed many more such hairs inside the vitrine. The marmoset was lowered into the glass box to retrieve the teapot. Having done so, it was then locked inside and eaten by the python. A noisy marmoset is a liability to a burglar after the act."

Colonel Cumberbutch intervened. "You agree the Sikh was in on the burglary?"

"Yes," replied Sherlock blandly, "but you won't find him quayside waiting to board a ship heading for the Bay of Bengal. After he used the marmoset to steal the teapot, he too became a liability. One of the Chinese triads would have taken care of him."

"Which triad?" Madame Fang's voice was as sharp as a stropped razor.

"You will discover that fact, Madame, when they fish his mutilated body out of the river. Each gang leaves their own special calling card. The gang that purchased the Yixing teapot from the thief will thus reveal itself."

He held the second hair in his fingers for all to see; or not; the black one with the greenish tinge. "Here is a hair from that tautonymous creature which can sometimes have a greenish tinge - *rattus rattus*; not fed to the python, but a common visitor to the Tiffin Tearoom of an evening to feast on cake crumbs. You will find more of these hairs underneath most tables and around the edges of the room. An unnecessary distraction to the case." He tossed the rat hair back on the floor.

I thought he was overdoing it a bit. It wasn't his best performance.

He pulled out the third hair; the ginger one. "Here I have a distinctive *ang-moh* from a typical British subject." He used the pejorative term for red hair and I blushed for the colonel; the insult was clearly aimed at him. "This ginger hair was found at the scene of the crime – there are others - and I see by the nicks on the neck of Colonel Cumberbutch that he has recently shaved, not this morning, the nicks are not fresh, but perhaps yesterday, thus his whiskers were shedding more than usual when he paid a visit to the Tiffin Tearoom last night."

"That's absurd!" scoffed the colonel. "I was still on the high seas last night, heading for the Malacca Strait."

40

"I doubt it," said Sherlock calmly. "You have laterite mud on your boots. It rained last night but by this morning the roads were dry. The only way you could have got red mud on your boots was if you walked out last night."

"Rubbish!" shouted the colonel. "This mud is weeks old. It sticks like glue. I haven't cleaned my boots since I left Singapore."

"Then how do you explain this?" Sherlock plucked a small shiny object out of his top pocket. "This is a piece of oyster shell button. I found this outside the hotel, but not in any spot where you walked, Colonel Cumberbutch. I saw as you leapt from your rickshaw and hurried inside the hotel and yet your broken button was found several yards away. I suggest you dropped it last night when you waited for your accomplice in the dark while eating a curry from a banana leaf. It is easy to check. My supposition is that it will be a perfect match for the broken button of your shirt."

"This is errant nonsense!" retorted the colonel, turning bright red. "Mr Holmes is jealous that I have solved the case and is inventing facts to suit his fancy! Next he will assert that Miss Luxi Gong was my accomplice!"

"I will assert no such thing. Miss Gong was sold to white slavers last night to stop her identifying you as the thief."

"Madness!" yelled the colonel.

"I notice you have several scratches on your right cheek and a vicious red bite mark on your left hand made by a small jaw; female. I assert she scratched and bit as you dragged her to a waiting rickshaw. It was she who broke your button in the struggle. In the process you ripped her dress. There was a scrap of silk under a discarded banana leaf in the forecourt. Easy to confirm. I have it here." He pulled out a fragment of green silk with a repeating golden dragon pattern.

Mr Soolem recognised it and gasped. "She had that pattern on her *changsan* yesterday!"

"If you tell us where she is being held, Colonel Cumberbutch, it may go easier for you at your trial," said Sherlock.

The colonel was apoplectic. "What trial! Your proof is nothing more than a broken button and a scrap of cloth! That will never stand up in a court of law!"

"I daresay things will go easier for you in Outram Prison than with the justice of the street after Madame Fang's triad discovers which gang you did business with. A matter of a few hours before the body of the Sikh is washed up. Shall we slice up that python now?" He gave Mr Soolem a nod to proceed.

"What about these grey pebbles?" shouted the colonel. "You must account for every fact in a case! You cannot cherry pick clues!"

"Oh, them," said Sherlock carelessly. "Devil's dung."

"What!" frothed the colonel, staring at the dull little marbles. "Devil's dung?"

"You found the devil's latrine. The shitting spot of the Tasmanian devil. In other words, you have proved my next case for me...Baffles."

My head was spinning. "The case of the Giant Rat of Singapore?" said I.

"Yes, Watson," returned my modest friend. "I have long suspected that the Giant Rat of Singapore is really a marsupial: the Tasmanian Devil. The black hair with the white tip is a positive sign. A quarter of all Tasmanian devils have a white patch on their chest. The shriek everyone heard last night adds confirmation. The cry of the Tasmanian devil is one of the most frightening sounds in existence. The hunt starts tomorrow. I believe the creature arrived by ship from Australia at about the time the Palm Court was being built. It will have hunkered down somewhere in the garden. Let's hope it was not a pregnant female." He turned to the gutted python. "Ah! What have we here? A marmoset not yet fully digested."

Colonel Bulwer Cumberbutch made a dash for the door but Madame Fang's dagger flew through the air. With a groan he fell.

"Don't worry," she hissed through tea-stained teeth. "He's not dead...not yet. The location of Miss Gong first. My precious teapot second. Then death by a thousand cuts." She turned to Holmes. "Please to accept my gratitude. Name your reward."

Sherlock bowed his head and requested a G&T with a wedge of lime. "Make that two!" he added with a throttling laugh.

Anna Lord's Top Ten:

1. The Hound of the Baskervilles
2. The Adventure of the Final Problem
3. The Adventure of the Greek Interpreter
4. The Adventure of the Dancing Men
5. A Scandal in Bohemia
6. The Adventure of the Illustrious Client
7. The Five Orange Pips
8. The Adventure of the Lion's Mane
9. The Adventure of the Red Headed League
10. The Adventure of the Crooked Man

'What is it, Holmes?'
'It's a lamppost, Watson.'

The Man on the Tor...Geri Schear

There's a man on the Tor who is watching

    The Hall and the terrible moor,

I wonder what plot he is hatching

    He's up to no good, I am sure.

Selden, the convict, is stalking

    And signalling them in the Hall,

Somebody knows, but ain't talking

    So we wait for disaster to fall.

The legend says terror is waiting

    For Baskerville's under a curse

Sir Henry can act deprecating

    But I've seen the Hound, and what's worse

I've heard its howling at midnight

      Heralding death to the haunted

When the moon stands at its full height

      And the power of evil's exalted.

Now evil is all we're foreseeing;

      The doctor found tracks on the ground

The marks of a man who was fleeing,

      And the prints of a gigantic hound.

The man on the Tor has the answers

      They say he's a threat to all foes

Preventing dark fate and disaster

      A consulting detective named Holmes.

But logic defeats superstition

      And Sherlock Holmes revealed all

The killer's dispatched to perdition

      And peace reigns o'er Baskerville Hall

Opening Lines......David Ruffle

Just think how much of literature could be improved with certain Holmesian additions. Consider these opening lines for instance. Feel free to play along and work out which books these come from and come up with some of your own!

"Please, sir, is this 221b Baker Street?" asked a ragged boy of the man who opened the door at which the omnibus left him.

"Christmas won't be Christmas without any presents," grumbled Sherlock Holmes, lying on the rug.

"It is a truth universally acknowledged, that a consulting detective in possession of a good fortune must not necessarily be in want of a wife."

"When Doctor Watson went to Baker Street to live with Sherlock Holmes, everybody said he was the most disagreeable-looking doctor ever seen."

"It was about eleven o'clock in the morning, mid-October, with the sun not shining and a look of hard wet rain in the clearness of the gutters of Baker Street."

"Stately, plump Mycroft Holmes came from the stairhead, bearing a bowl of lather on which a mirror and a razor lay crossed. A yellow dressing gown, ungirdled, was sustained gently behind him by the mild morning air. He held the bowl aloft and intoned: ----*Introibo ad altare Dei.*"

"Someone must have traduced Doctor Watson, for without having done anything wrong he was arrested one fine morning."

"Sherlock Holmes and Dr Watson sat one morning in the window-bay of 221b Baker Street, working and talking."

"During the whole of a dull, dark, and soundless day in the autumn of the year, when the clouds hung oppressively low in the heavens, I had been passing alone, on horseback, through a singularly dreary tract of country; and at length found myself, as the shades of the evening drew on, within view of the melancholy Baskerville Hall. I know not how it was - but, with the first glimpse of the building, a sense of insufferable gloom pervaded my spirit."

"The manager had no business to do it," said Holmes, "no business at all. He promised us south rooms with a view close together, instead of which here are north rooms, looking into a courtyard, and a long way apart. Oh, Watson!"

"Holmes knew, before he had been in Brighton three hours, that they meant to murder him."

"My dear wife Mary and I have just been a week in our new home, 64 Queen Anne Street--a nice six-roomed residence, not counting basement, with a front-breakfast parlour."

"Sherlock Holmes's jaw was long and bony, his chin a jutting v under the more flexible v of his mouth. His nostrils curved back to make another, smaller v. His yellow-grey eyes were horizontal. The v motif was picked up again by thickish brows rising outward from twin creases above a hooked nose, and his pale brown hair grew down--from high flat temples--in a point on his forehead. He looked rather pleasantly like a blond satan."

He said to his colleague: "Yes, Watson?"

"I was leaning against the bar in a saloon on Oxford Street, waiting for Mary to finish her Christmas shopping, when a girl got up from the table where she had been sitting with three other people and came over to see me. She was small and blonde, and whether you looked at her face or at her body in powder-blue sports clothes, the result was satisfactory. "Aren't you Doctor Watson?" she asked."

"When Sherlock Holmes smiled, the corners of his mouth spread till they were within an unimportant distance of his ears, his eyes were reduced to chinks, and diverging wrinkles appeared round them, extending upon his countenance like the rays in a rudimentary sketch of the rising sun."

"Moriarty was dead: to begin with. There is no doubt whatever about that. The register of his burial was signed by the clergyman, the clerk, the undertaker, and the chief mourner. Holmes signed it. And Holmes's name was good upon 'Change, for anything he chose to put his hand to.

"Old Moriarty was as dead as a door-nail."

"Last night I dreamt I went to Shoscombe Old Place again."

Deceptive Appearances....Margaret Walsh

It was hard to believe that the man walking slowly towards me was the greatest mind in Britain, if not the world. The aforesaid mind was housed in a body so corpulent it was reminiscent of a pregnant hippopotamus.

He walked up to the desk I was standing at and murmured, "Is the Stranger's Room free tonight, William?"

"Yes, Mr Holmes."

"Good. Please have a table for three set. My brother and his companion will be joining me for supper. What's available, do you know?"

"Roast beef with all the trimmings, sir. With a fine fish soup to start, bread and butter pudding for afters, and I was told to tell you that the kitchen now has that excellent French blue cheese you like to go with the port."

Mycroft Holmes fairly beamed at me. "Excellent. A fine supper for us all." He headed for the Stranger's Room, and I headed for the kitchens to let them know what was required.

I suppose I should introduce myself. My name is William Smith and I am a doorman/flunkey at the Diogenes Club. Don't bother looking it up. You won't have heard of it. It's very exclusive and very eccentric. You probably won't have heard of Mycroft Holmes either, and he would like it kept that way. You will have heard of his brother though, the great Sherlock Holmes, and his friend and biographer, Doctor John Watson. Damn them all to Hell! The conversation flowed around the small table as I poured the port to end the meal.

"I assure you, Mycroft, my source is reliable."

"I'm sure it is, Sherlock, but, really, who would want to kill me?"

"Apart from almost everyone who knows you?"

"Holmes!" Doctor Watson, barked. "You're confusing your brother with yourself!"

Sherlock Holmes scowled at his friend, whose eyes twinkled with amusement. Mycroft Holmes chuckled richly. "Good shot, my dear doctor. A very good shot indeed."

As I poured port into the glass laid out for Mycroft, the doctor gestured with his fork, knocking the glass to the ground, spilling the fortified wine. "Oh dear..."

"It is fine, doctor. No harm is done."

"Except to the carpet."

"We've had blood on this carpet, Sherlock. A little wine isn't going to worry the cleaning staff. Any more than it worries you."

The doctor passed his glass to Mycroft. "Here. Do have mine. I haven't touched it."

Mycroft took the glass with a nod of thanks, sipping the port thoughtfully. "I understand, in theory, that certain foreign powers might want me out of the way. But at this point in time I do not see for whom it would be advantageous to have me removed from the playing field."

"My source suggests that the Tzar of all the Russias is looking to spread his wings. You are a known peace maker, brother dear, with you out of the way there would be no-one to keep Britain and Germany from each other's throats."

"And whilst we were fighting," Doctor Watson added, "The Tzar would take the opportunity to snip a little land away from the Kaiser."

"Interesting theory." Mycroft raised his glass and studied the fluid within. "Excellent vintage, this. William?"

"Yes sir?"

"Tell the cellar man to order as many cases of this as he can. It's quite a robust little drop. Reminiscent of a good Artillery port."

"Yes sir." I turned away just as Doctor Watson managed to upset the finger bowl next to Mycroft. Water cascaded onto the floor. How did a man that clumsy get to be a doctor?

"Really, Watson, I simply cannot take you anywhere!" Sherlock Holmes openly smirked.

"Never mind, I'll just use a napkin instead of the water to clean my hands."

"Allow me, sir." I leaned over Mycroft Holmes to lay a clean napkin on his lap, I surreptitiously flexed my right wrist to release the thin bladed knife concealed there…and froze. Something cold and metallic was pressed under my right ear.

"Do not even think about it." The voice was ice cold.

The next moment I was swung away from Mycroft, my arms pinioned behind me, and handcuffs slapped around my wrists by Sherlock Holmes.

I turned my head and looked to the source of that cold voice. Doctor Watson stood there, a revolver in his hand that was pointed straight at my head. Gone was the jovial dinner companion, and the amiable buffoon. This man was more than capable of pulling the trigger and it showed in every line of his body and in the cold light in his eyes. I was shoved into an abandoned chair.

Sherlock Holmes looked sharply at me. "It's not the Tzar who wants Mycroft dead, though, it's the Kaiser. That twaddle was for your benefit. "

Mycroft Holmes smiled benignly at me. "I am curious as to why the Kaiser thought he could get away with killing me. He hasn't anyone in his service nearly intelligent enough to outwit my brother on one of his rare off days, let alone myself." He took a meditative sip of the port, and glanced at his brother.

Sherlock took up the thread again. "We knew within hours of the German government's approach to you what was happening, William, or should I say Wilhelm? Your mother is German, is she not?"

I looked away and did not reply.

Doctor Watson shook his head. "Surely you realised that all members of the Diogenes Club staff are watched?"

That was news to me. I looked quickly at Mycroft. He nodded. "With the membership including a number of politicians, wealthy businessmen, and more than a few peers, naturally security is a high priority."

Sherlock Holmes spoke again. "We kept an eye on the roster. Once we knew you would be working tonight it was child's play to organize this little charade." He smiled briefly at Doctor Watson. "My good friend is usually nowhere near as clumsy as he was tonight." Holmes turned his attention back to me. "I know you were merely to deliver the two poisons. Your co-conspirator at the German embassy is at this moment explaining himself to the King, prior to being shipped back to Germany in ignominy. No doubt to his death, as the Kaiser cannot abide any failure, except his own. A pity, Mycroft will miss playing him at chess, and a lass in the kitchen will miss his gallant attentions. As to the your part in the matter…the sticky stem on one of the port glasses told you which glass had had poison painted in its interior, and the finger bowl with the 'X' scratched into its base told you the same poison had been spread there. The blade at your wrist was simply a contingency plan in case something went wrong."

He sipped his own port. "You're right, Mycroft. This really is an excellent port."

"I shall see that a case is delivered to Baker Street tomorrow."

Sherlock Holmes looked back to me. "It was fiendish in its simplicity. The robustness of the port would disguise any taste, and if Mycroft didn't drink the port, he would wash his fingers prior to eating the cheese, and that pungent blue cheese that he so loves would, once again, serve to disguise the taste."

The door to the Stranger's Room opened. Three burly men entered, and, at Mycroft's nod, hauled me from my seat, and out of the room.

I sit here now in a cell in the Tower of London, of all places. I haven't been tried. Mycroft advised the King against it. My 'treason' is proven by my own actions, and he doesn't want to precipitate a war between Britain and Germany. That will come. As surely as the sun will rise tomorrow, war will come.

I die today. I will be hanged by the neck, though at least my body will be given to my mother for burial. Doctor Watson assured me of this. He demanded it of Mycroft Holmes, and Mycroft consented.

I thought it was hard to believe that the greatest mind in Britain lurked in the bulk that is Mycroft Holmes. But I learned something else that night. That Doctor John H. Watson has the most deceptive appearance of all. An iron resolve and a great heart in the body of a gentle and unassuming man.

Margaret Walsh's TopTen:

1. The Hound of the Baskervilles – *Watson gets to be the detective for most of the book. And one the most twisted plots ACD ever came up with.*

2. A Study in Scarlet – *The first meeting of Holmes & Watson. "You have been in Afghanistan, I perceive" still sends shivers down my spine.*

3. Silver Blaze – *loved for 'the curious incident of the dog in the nightime'.*

4. The Adventure of the Empty House – *Holmes returns and Watson passes out!*

5. The Adventure of Charles Augustus Milverton – *a favourite because of the scene with Lestrade at the end.*

6. The Adventure of the Red Headed League – *One of the oddest cases to come along, but also one of the most entertaining.*

7. The Adventure of the Speckled Band – *Murder by serpent. What's not to like?*

8. A Scandal in Bohemia – *Irene Adler. What other reason do I need?*

9. The Man with the Twisted Lip – *Fabulous murder case that turns out to be something else entirely.*

10. The Adventure of the Three Garridebs – *We get to see just how strong this wonderful friendship is.*

The Grayford School Mystery...Danielle Gastineau

When I was younger, about six or seven I must have been, I asked my grandmother, the renowned Mrs Hudson, why Mr. Holmes often seemed to let some criminals go free. She would explain that not all people who commit crimes are as bad as they are made out to be and often there is a reason behind why they committed the crime. Some do it for attention or they are in some sort of trouble they can't get out of, these people may have even tried to seek help but were never given any so they turned to crime to solve their problem. This of course does not exonerate them from their actions although it may explain such actions. Mr Holmes, she explained was a merciful man, but not a man with whom to take liberties.

I understood this much better several years later when a series of robberies had taken place at my school. Every year my school undertook to hold a clothing drive for the poor, in which we would collect old clothes from families around our neighbourhood. Local churches set up collection points and people such as my parents would put a space in their shop where people can drop their donations off.

My school was Grayford School named after the man who built it Mr. Joseph Grayford, he and his wife believed all children, no matter what their background may be, had the right a decent education. The school was housed in large two storey brick building in Kensington, each year there was at least sixty to one hundred children between the ages of five and sixteen years of age who would pass through its doors. The school boasted several very well appointed classrooms, an art and music room, a sparsely filled, but very useful library, a kitchen which smelled permanently of cabbage and a canteen which shared the same aroma.

My fellow pupils and classmates were all aged thirteen or fourteen and this year it was my class who had the responsibility of collecting clothing for the poor. This particular day my teacher, Mrs. James a tall, slender lady with brown hair and brown eyes, walked into the classroom trying to hide the fact she had been crying. Mrs. James was one of my favourite teachers and before my friend Dawn and I left for our cabbage soup lunch we were determined to ask her why she looked so upset.

My friend Dawn McNamee who had dark red hair and green eyes had decided to speak first. Dawn and I had been the best of friends since we could walk, she and her parents had moved to London from County Cork in Ireland when she was about a year old and her father was a baker and had landed a job at my parent's bakery, they lived next door to the bakery while my parents and I lived above the bakery.

"Are you all right, Mrs. James?" Dawn asked.

"No, Dawn. The clothing we collected," Miss James said, sighing. "It has been stolen."

"What?" I cried. "Why would anyone be so mean?"

"I wish I could answer that," Miss James sighed.

~*~ ~*~ ~*~ ~*~ ~*~ ~*~ ~*~ ~*~

"How could someone do such a thing?" my grandmother said to me that same evening, echoing my own words. "Stealing from the poor. What is the world coming to?"

"We worked so hard to collect all of it too," I said, sadly.

"I know, Molly," replied my grandmother smiling and handing me a cup of tea which in her eyes was a cure for all ills.

"Mrs. Hudson!" came the strident voice of Mr. Holmes from the upstairs landing.

"Can you find out what he wants? I am getting dinner ready. He has to realise I cannot always be at his beck and call."

59

"Yes, I will." I replied and headed up the seventeen steps to the first floor.

On arriving I found Doctor Watson sitting in his chair reading his newspaper and Mr. Holmes was busy at his chemistry table, test tubes full of all manner of coloured fluids. He motioned me to come and watch and I observed as he poured a solution into a small bottle that was filled with green liquid. There was a pop and a puff and a sudden plume of smoke made me jump.

"Where's your grandmother?" Holmes asked me as he continued his dabbling.

"She is preparing dinner. She asked me to see what you wanted." She also said...well...perhaps...not."

He looked at me inquisitively. "Hmm. I only wanted her to bring Watson and me some tea," he said.

"I'll ask her," I said and started out the door then turned back to them "Wait, maybe you can help me with something." I turned back towards them.

"What do you need my help with?" Holmes asked putting the bottles safely in their place and turning his attention to me.

"A case," I told him.

~*~ ~*~ ~*~ ~*~ ~*~ ~*~ ~*~ ~*~

The very next morning Mr. Holmes and Dr. Watson arrived at my school to speak to Mr. Grayford. Mr. Grayford was an elderly man in his sixties, his office was medium sized with several book shelves, a desk with two chairs in front of that desk. When I told Mr. Holmes what had happened he wanted to help, I asked him about his other cases he was working on and he told me they were coming to a conclusion and he would help me out with this little problem.

The room where the clothing was kept was in a storage room at the back of the school behind the kitchens, the only way to get in was to go through the front of the school and down the main hallway and through the kitchens. After a quick look around Holmes, so I learned later, informed Mr Grayford that the person or persons responsible must have remained hidden the night of the theft and broken into the room and then left through the window. He declared the miscreant to be a child, the footprints on the windowsill being small in size. Holmes asked that Mr Grayford take note as to who was absent, Mr. Grayford didn't even want to believe a student would be involved but he agreed to do it. Another theory was expounded that someone had sneaked in while classes were in session and went unnoticed.

"Did they find anything?" I asked Mrs. James when she entered the classroom. She didn't want to share the findings with the other children so bent down and whispered in my ear.

"No, Molly not yet, but with Sherlock Holmes on the case I am sure we will have news soon," she replied, smiling.

"Can we hold another clothing drive, Mrs. James?" another student asked.

"I think that is a lovely idea if we have the time to do so," Mrs. James answered. Mrs. James looked around and began her normal head count and a student named Juliette was not in class.

"Has anyone seen Juliette Martin?" Mrs. James asked, but no one answered.

After school had ended, Mrs. James wrote a note for me to take to Mr. Holmes, she had a meeting to attend with Mr. Grayford and the rest of the teaching staff so she could not go with me. I knew little about Juliette, only that her parents were well off and she lived in Kensington not far from the school. I told Dr. Watson and Holmes that I had never really had much to do with her although I did have tea and cakes with her one evening.

"Is this the house, Molly?" Mr. Holmes asked me as we drove up in the cab, it was a prominent three storey home faced in red brick with symmetrical sash windows.

"Yes," I answered.

"Please stay in the cab, Molly," Holmes said as he and Dr. Watson climbed out. I watched as they walked up to the door which Holmes rapped loudly on. After a delay of several minutes an older woman answered the door and I heard him ask if the lady of the house was in. The older lady clearly being a servant.

"What are you doing here?" Juliette said suddenly, thrusting her head, with its tight blonde curls, into the cab.

"Mr. Holmes and Dr. Watson had to make a call and I am waiting for them," I told her.

"Why have they come to my house?" Juliette asked.

"Someone robbed the school, all the clothing we collected are gone."I told her.

"So you blame me, is that it?" Juliette asked in an offended tone.

"I didn't blame anyone," I replied. "Mrs. James prepared a list of students who were not in attendance today and you were the only one."

"You should have them leave," Juliette said, heatedly.

"What's wrong?" I asked her. "Mr. Holmes can help you if you need it."

"Nothing's wrong. Just go, the two of them being here will only make things worse." Juliette said and looked down the street and appeared to get really tense. "I have to go."

Juliette suddenly hid behind some tall bushes when an older man with straggly, grey hair and mean looked to him walked up to the house, he was wearing a black suit and a top hat, he looked towards me and walked up and walked up to the cab.

"Why are you in front of my house, child?" the man, who appeared very agitated, asked. I saw Juliette hide herself behind the *leylandii*. Why is she afraid of you? Answer me child," he said, angrily.

It was me who was the scared one at that moment.

"She's waiting for us," Holmes said, coming up silently behind the man. "We are just visiting your neighbour."

The man said nothing other than muttering something unintelligible under his breath as he let himself into the house Holmes and Watson had just left.

"Who is that?" Dr. Watson asked.

"I don't know" I said. I told them about Juliette coming up to the cab and hiding when the man came.

"The father," Holmes said. "There was a family painting in the sitting room which displayed such a patriarch."

"He's scary," I said, still a little shaken by the encounter.

"Something's going on in that house, you mark my words," Dr. Watson said.

"Maybe we can get Wiggins and the other Irregulars to spy on them," I suggested.

"An excellent idea, young lady." Holmes said.

"It seems a lot of fuss for the loss of a few old clothes," Watson interjected.

"Really, Watson, Molly has put her faith in us. Are you proposing to let her down?"

The good doctor looked at me and managed to somehow both nod and shake his head at the same time.

I told them I would go and give Wiggins the location and instructions on what to do. After leaving the house in Kensington I found Wiggins at his usual spot near the entrance to Hyde Park where he loved to watch the world go by. I gave him the message and a few shillings from Mr. Holmes. Later that night Wiggins and two other boys went to the house. I suggested that they hide themselves where Juliette had earlier, it being very effective.

As soon as they arrived they heard shouting and Wiggins looked inside the window and saw a woman sitting on a couch and crying and an older man could be heard lecturing her about her place in their home. The woman started telling him about knowing about the debt they were in and she had threatened to leave if he didn't change his ways and he again let her know she could never leave him. He would not allow it.

"What are you doing?" Wiggins heard a voice. The boys saw a girl who they assumed was Juliette from the description I had given them.

"Mr. Sherlock Holmes sent us," Wiggins said.

"To spy on my family?" Juliette said.

"No, my friend Molly's school was robbed and if you know anything about you should tell us now."

"I don't know anything and if you stay here any longer I'll summon a constable."

Wiggins and the boys could not imagine this slip of a girl summoning anyone let alone a constable, but they duly left. Juliette went back inside. She found her mother in the sitting room alone her. She loved her mother and hated that she had to steal to make sure she could keep her home. She closed the door and saw her father walk to his study, he noticed her and didn't say word and when he got into the study, simply slammed the door. She just then realised the boys were right, she had to speak up.

"Mother, I must speak." Juliette said.

"I thought you were upstairs."

"Let's go to America and Aunt Colleen," Juliette said.

"Your father will never let us leave," her mother replied.

"I stole the clothing for us and it wasn't right, we need help, Mother and if that detective can help us we must let him." Juliette told her.

"But you may be convicted as a thief," Mrs. Martin said, tearfully. "And whatever happens, your father will cut us off without a penny to our name if we leave."

"I don't care, living on the streets would be better than this."

"You are right, we will go and see this Mr. Holmes in the morning."

The next morning Mrs. Martin and Juliette left for Baker Street, she had told her husband she was going to take her daughter to do some shopping in the city. When they arrived at Baker Street Mr. Holmes asked Billy the page boy to send a telegram to both Mrs. James and Mr. Grayford and ask them to come to 221b Baker Street.

"I asked my daughter steal the clothing," Mrs. Martin confessed. "We needed the money by selling some of them and keeping some for ourselves."

"Why?" Holmes asked.

"My husband's gambling debts have brought us to this sorry state. He has taken several loans from the bank and the lenders sent him messages that if he didn't pay up they would take everything."

Mrs Martin broke down in tears. Juliette did her very best to console her. Doctor Watson took the step of ringing for my grandmother to help out with a reviving pot of tea. By the time Mrs Martin had composed herself Mr Grayford and Mrs James had arrived and Holmes had recounted the situation to them.

"How much money does your husband owe?" Mr. Grayford asked.

"Over ten thousand pounds, I believe, although it may be higher. I don't want to lose my home, my daughter loves attending your school and don't want to see her lose her chance of a fine education."

"I'm sorry Mr. Grayford, Mrs. James, really I am sorry." Juliette said, tears rolling down her cheeks.

"I can't live this way anymore and I can't live with a man who does not care about what he is doing to his family," Mrs. Martin said, "I can't leave him, he won't let us."

"Why didn't you ask for help?" Mrs. James asked.

"My father," Juliette said, "is very controlling."

"I think this act of theft can be forgiven," Mrs. James said. "We can always hold another clothing drive and Juliette is a good student, she has never caused trouble before and I am sure she will never again transgress."

"I agree," Mr. Grayford said, with a smile. "And I won't press charges."

"What about my husband and his debt and the shame he has caused us, he will be upset with me if he finds out I came here," Mrs. Martin said.

"Do you have any family in London?" Dr. Watson asked.

"In America, we have my aunt, my mother's sister." Juliette said.

"You will go to America," Mr. Holmes stated.

"What about my husband" Mrs. Martin asked. "He won't allow us to leave and I have no hope of obtaining a divorce and besides we have no money for a passage to America. Our plight is as bad as it was before."

"My brother has some friends in the courts" Holmes told her. "He owes me a favour, so do not worry about a divorce. It will be arranged with no regard to the will of your husband. My advice is to go home and begin the process of packing. If you leave me the address of your sister, I will ensure she receives a cable telling her of your imminent arrival."

"But, as I have just said, we have no funds."

"Mrs Martin, we have something we like to call the Baker Street Emergency Purse, do we not, Watson?"

"Er...yes of course. It's just as Holmes says, Mrs Martin."

"Thank you, gentlemen. What will become of my husband?"

"He had made his bed, I propose he lies on it. Start your new life and do not look back," Holmes replied.

Thanks to Mycroft's help the courts eventually allowed for Juliette's mother to get her divorce. By that Juliette and her mother were already in America. Before they departed, the entire school threw Juliette a goodbye party and Juliette promised to try and keep in touch, she also told me to thank my friend Wiggins, which I gladly did.

"Do you think they will be all right?" I asked Mr. Holmes a few days after they left. My parents were out with some friends and I was at my grandmothers in his sitting room working on my homework at the table.

"Yes, I am sure of it, Molly," Holmes replied from behind the book he was reading.

"Thank you for taking the case, not that it was really a case."

"It upset you," he said, finally putting his book down. "And that upset me."

"I did enjoy going on the investigation with you. Thank you for letting me come along"

"You are very welcome, young lady," he said, smiling, then returned his attention to his book.

Danielle Gastineau's Top Ten:

1. The Hound of the Baskervilles
2. A Study in Scarlet
3. The Adventure of the Yellow Face
4. The Sign of Four
5. The Adventure of the Blue Carbuncle
6. The Adventure of Charles Augustus Milverton
7. The Adventure of the Illustrious Client
8. The Red-Headed League
9. A Scandal in Bohemia
10. Silver Blaze

'What is it, Holmes?'
'It's a piece of paper, Watson.'

The Affair of the Mother's Return...David Marcum

It was in the first year of my marriage that I received one of those laconic messages from my friend, Mr. Sherlock Holmes, requesting my presence at our old lodgings in the northern end of Baker Street. As my practice was never very engaging, especially that day, and my wife's health was causing no concern that day, I decided to go. Shaking off my mid-morning drowsiness, and donning my coat against the autumn chill, I departed.

The walk from Paddington was unusually pleasant, and I had time to ponder upon our recent trip to Edinburgh, and that little matter of the Robert Burns Cameo at the recently opened Scottish National Portrait Gallery, wherein an innocent substitution of an obviously inferior copy had led to a suicide, a wedding, and a promise to the Lord Advocate that Holmes and I would never again return to the Gallery again without a specific invitation.

Letting myself into the entryway at No. 221, I paused for a moment to listen. The house was quiet, and I decided that Mrs. Hudson must be out, as she was normally quite alert as to the comings and goings through her front door.

I began to climb the steps, aware that if Holmes were upstairs, he would hear me and recognise who I was from my characteristic limp – although now much less noticeable than when I first mounted these steps years earlier. Pausing for a moment on the turn of the stairs, I looked out the landing window into the rear yard, and the plane tree growing there. It had never been a very healthy fellow, even at the best of times, and it had never quite recovered from when Holmes had poured the end results of one of his chemical experiments into the soil nearby, indicating that the contents, used to poison a banker, were far too foul for London's sewers.

With a sigh, I shook my head and continued up the steps. Knocking on the closed sitting room door and then turning the knob without waiting for a response, I stepped inside to find Holmes curled into his chair, his head wreathed in pipe smoke. With a languid wave, he silently gestured toward my old armchair.

I settled into the well-worn cushions and glanced around the room. As usual, it was filled with relics of my friend's cases, an ever-changing collection of the bizarre, the random, and the unexplained. Since my last visit, only a few days earlier, I observed the addition of some sort of tribal figurine, stalwartly but ineffectively anchoring a slumping pile of papers on the floor beside the dining table, and a bottle of reddish liquid, in which there're floated what suspiciously resembled a severed human great toe. I wanted to ask about the significance of these new items before Holmes had the chance to progress to some new bit of business, thereby losing interest in them. Before I could clear my throat to speak, however, he was straightening in his chair and tossing me a letter.

Reaching for a pinch of tobacco, and without a word of greeting, he said, "I would value your insight on this little matter."

I picked up the sheet that had landed perfectly in my lap. It consisted of a single leaf of thick and somewhat expensive stationary. Noting that it had been folded once, I asked, "Was there an envelope?"

"Good, Watson!" replied Holmes. "You are examining all aspects of the item before jumping to conclusions. Our friends at the Yard would have simply read the thing."

"Not altogether unreasonable," I said wryly. I glanced at the sheet. It was a short message, written only on one side, with a broad-tipped pen. Right handed, with a very calm and even line, showing no signs of hurry or emotional distress. I tilted the paper back and forth toward the fading afternoon light from the window behind Holmes. No watermark, and it was a true black ink, not something watered down that one might find at a bank, hotel, or other public location. I checked...there was no odour, such as tobacco or incense, to provide any information. The stiffness of the paper, as well as the apparent quality of the ink, indicated a person who was not necessarily of means, but certainly comfortably off.

"The envelope?" I repeated.

He picked it up from the small octagonal table by his chair. I had already seen it there, and suspected that it matched the missive in my hand.

This time he leaned forward to hand it to me, perhaps not trusting his ability to repeat the perfect toss of the letter, possibly due to the envelope's flap disrupting its aerodynamic symmetry. I glanced at him as I took possession of it, and saw a slight smile on his face, and I knew that he knew what I was thinking.

The envelope resembled the stationary, and the address on the front was written by the same pen, and with the same hand. There was no return address or postage stamp, indicating that in some way the message had been hand delivered.

Finally I turned my attention to the contents of the letter.

Dear Mr. Holmes, (it read)

I am taking the liberty to request an appointment with you today at 10 a.m. (I glanced at the mantle clock – ten minutes until the hour.) *to lay a matter before you concerning my parents. Perhaps you have heard of the unfortunate Leland and Sarah Cole. I had believed the affair to have been long settled, but recent events have served to arouse my curiosity.*

Unless I receive word to the contrary, I shall plan upon laying this matter before you.

Very best regards,

Andrew Cole

"And how was this letter delivered?"

"A commissionaire. Mrs. Hudson didn't recognise him. If it becomes important, we can certainly track him down. However, the fellow will be here in just a few moments, and the question will likely be answered in due course."

I glanced toward the envelope. "How did he expect to receive word if he didn't provide his address?"

"Quite right. He is young."

"You know him, then?"

"Rather, I know of him by knowing of his parents."

"The letter is so calmly written. It's curious he didn't notice that error."

"It is calm, but I suspect that the emotions related to the situation run deep."

"And his parents?"

He reached toward one of his scrapbooks, standing against the mantel beneath his Persian slipper. I had noticed it there, but had credited it no importance in relation to this matter, as there were so many other haphazard items scattered hither and yon about the room. Handing it to me, he added, "The page is marked."

Describing it as a "page" was charitable. Holmes's scrapbooks were collections of news clippings, brochures, programs, labels, and photographs, mixed in with the occasional indiscriminate glassine envelope of ash, tissue, or a hundred, nay, a thousand other possibilities. Residing on a sagging shelf mounted to the wall between the fireplace and Holmes's bedroom, these commonplace books were the primary annex to Holmes's brain attic. He spent a great deal of time updating them, culling articles from newspapers, and making annotations throughout about this or that item, or an individual who had come to his attention and was marked down for greater things, in the sense that the person was putting his first steps on a path leading to the gallows.

After having a small packet fall to my lap containing what appeared to be a fine collection of mismatched small animal claws, I found the items to which my attention had been directed: Namely, a clipped and tidy stack of newspaper articles, now yellowed with age, relating to Leland Cole.

Taking them out, I closed the book, such as it was, and stood it on the floor beside my own chair. "You could have simply handed me the clippings," I said, beginning to quickly read through them.

There were half-a-dozen, all from mid-1880, except for one dated early the following year, specifically February 1881. Although presenting different perspectives, the facts of the case were rather clear. Cole had been a rising constable with Scotland Yard when the Turf Fraud Scandal of '77 led to the formation of the CID the next year. During the reorganization, he had been promoted to Detective Sergeant, a position held until he was forced to resign three years later. Apparently, he had been implicated in the theft of a great deal of gold coins from a group of bank robbers who were all found dead in a Bermondsey lodging house. The gold was never found, but it was suspected that Cole had been in league with the men, killed them, and then taken the loot. While no firm proof was ever found, his credibility within the Force was shattered, and he was released from his position.

The final article from 1881 simply indicated that no new clues had been found, either toward identifying and locating the killer or the stolen money, although there was the obligatory statement that "the police are following certain leads".

"The evidence must have been quite strong against the man," I said. "'Innocent until proven guilty' didn't save his job."

"I understand that the feeling was that his connection to the matter was well established, if not proven. As you know, I was out of England during that portion of 1880, so I had no opportunity to consult on the matter. When I arrived home later that autumn and set about catching up on all that I had missed, this came to my attention, and I mentioned it to Lestrade, but he was quite understandably reluctant to open old wounds."

"Even if it meant resolving the question?"

"Your confidence in me is noted, Watson, but in those earlier days, the official force was much more inclined to see me as a useful amateur rather than a prized confidante."

I tapped the letter from Cole with a finger. "You say that Cole is young?"

"Yes. He would have been about sixteen at the time of the murders, as I recall."

"Making him about twenty-six or twenty-seven now. Not so young. I was nearly twenty-eight at Maiwand, and you were also already well established by that age."

"True. Perhaps I did err in crediting his epistolary *faux pas* to simple youth and inexperience. Another question to ask him, as I hear the bell ringing. Excuse me, Watson, while I go let him in. Mrs. Hudson is visiting her sister, and I am left alone to pilot the domestic ship."

And so saying, he made his way downstairs. I heard the usual business of the door opening and closing, removal of a coat, murmured conversation, and then the return of the detective with his client.

We were introduced, and I had a chance to observe Andrew Cole as he settled into the basket chair across from the fire. He acknowledged the lack of available tea or coffee, and waved away an offer of something stronger. He was in his mid-twenties, as expected, a big fellow with longish blonde hair, almost Byronic in its style. He was broad-shouldered, but seemed to have inherited it rather than developed it from hard work. His hands were well-manicured, and maintained for work with pen and paper, rather than tools. He had a frank open countenance, but it was marred by worry lines between his brows, and he sat forward on the chair instead of relaxing. He glanced at his note on the table beside my chair and, looking back and forth between us, began to apologize.

"I realized just moments after it left my hand that I had neglected to provide a return address, should this appointment be inconvenient." He glanced toward me. "Mr. Holmes explained downstairs that this time is acceptable, but I never meant to foist myself upon you so impolitely."

"We *had* noticed that you had neglected to tell us where to reach you," replied Holmes, his fingers steepled before his eyes.

Andrew Cole nodded. "I wrote and rewrote what I would say before carefully copying the final missive, but I never thought about something so basic."

"It is of no matter. You are correct that I recall the matter of your father, but I didn't know of any related involvement by your mother, as mentioned in the letter."

"I'm afraid that there is more to the affair than was ever made public, and my mother's reputation must have been as compromised as my father's, if only by association."

Holmes gestured at Cole to continue.

"As you may remember, my father was a Detective Sergeant in 1877, and those were good times for us. We had a small home, and while there was never much to spare, to be sure, we were warm and well-fed, and I felt safe. Then came the troubles.

"I'll admit that I was ignorant at the time of much that occurred. I was aware of a tension that hadn't existed before, and my mother and father, who had previously been much devoted to one another, now shared harsh words, often in whispers as they tried to protect me from knowing exactly what was happening. Only later was I able to force my father to tell me the story – at least, his version of it, as I'm sure to this day that he held back many important facts.

"According to him, on the night of the incident he had finished his duties and was returning home. It was quite late, and as he passed by a building, one of many in a row of darkened structures, his instincts as a former constable were aroused when he saw an unlocked door, standing partly open. (Much was made at the time that the building where this occurred was nowhere near the direct route between the police station where he worked and our home, and he never adequately explained exactly why he was actually in that area.)

"He knocked and received no answer. Entering the building, he perceived a single light coming from a back room, when the rest of the building was in darkness. Proceeding cautiously down the hallway, he entered a kitchen, lit by a single gas-lamp. He told me that the harsh light horrifyingly highlighted the three bodies lying on the floor, each of them dead and with their throats cut.

"As you'll recall, it was later determined that all of them had apparently been made unconscious by an opiate that was found in the stew that all three had eaten. The pot was still on the stove, and it contained more than enough of the narcotic to have put a dozen men to sleep. Apparently whoever had done so had then taken the opportunity to kill them unhindered.

"My father instantly recognized the three men as members of the Oak Ridge Gang, as all of them had been sought for the past couple of weeks following the robbery of the funds being accumulated by the Close Brothers for the formation of their bank."

Holmes nodded. "I recall that the theft wasn't widely reported, as the victims didn't want to undermine confidence in their upcoming financial endeavour."

"So I understand. In any case, the gold was never recovered."

"And your father," added Holmes, "was accused of taking advantage of the situation at best, and possibly of being involved in the theft."

"Yes. The official theory, although he was never charged, was that he was somehow in league with the Wards, the father and two sons, and that he had gone to meet them at that out-of-the-way house at the end of his working day. As you probably know, by the time he sounded the alarm, it was several hours after the end of his shift, and he was unable to account for either his time in between or his reasons for being in that area."

"And it was thought," I said, catching up, "that he went there for the meeting, put the men to sleep, killed them, moved the gold, only to then return and sound the alarm."

"Exactly, Doctor."

"But that makes no sense!" I exclaimed. "If he had no known connections to these men, he could have killed them and gotten away with the money without ever returning and sounding the alarm, thus trapping himself in that gyre."

"The reasoning power of the Yard," said Holmes wryly, "especially in those days, left a great deal to be desired. You've seen it a hundred times yourself, Watson. How often do they seek the simplest solution, bending facts to fit their theories?"

"Sometimes the simplest solution *is* the best," I said. "You've referred to Occam's Razor yourself, Holmes. And I've found in medicine that rare is rare and common is common."

"And stupid is stupid. However, in this case, it would have been uncommonly stupid indeed for Mr. Cole to have allowed himself to become more involved than he already had to be, even assuming that he was guilty." Holmes turned to our visitor. "Do you have any more information? Such as what happened after your father was drummed out of the Force without more substantial evidence of his guilt?"

"Nothing for certain, Mr. Holmes. As I said, at first I wasn't even aware of a problem. I have no recollection of the specific day when this would have happened. Back then, I slept quite soundly through the nights and hadn't many cares in the world. It was only over the course of the next days and weeks that I became aware of the increasing tension. My father and mother began to argue, although trying to hide it from me. It escalated to the point that finally, after a few weeks, my mother declared that she was leaving. Only then, when she was gone, did my father explain, in a very simplified way, what had happened and what was suspected of him. He was a broken man, and the fact that his own wife apparently believed the accusations against him only served as the final nail.

"And your mother left you there with him?" I asked, somewhat shocked.

"Exactly, Watson!" cried Holmes. "Quite unusual. Unheard of, as a matter of fact. That alone raises this matter to a different level." Turning back toward young Andrew Cole, he asked. "Why, now? What has happened that you've decided to consult me, after all this time? Has some new development occurred?"

"It has, Mr. Holmes. I have seen my mother!"

"And that is unusual because . . . ."

"Because I hadn't seen her since she left, back in 1880."

"What?" I asked. "You've had no contact with her whatsoever since that time?"

"No, Doctor. Following her departure, my father lost his job with the Force. He was able to obtain work as a groom at the estate of Lord Belving, in Surrey. My father had once done him a good turn, and it hadn't been forgotten. I spent the rest of my childhood, what little there was of it, there on the estate. Lord Belving, having no children of his own, took an interest in me and saw to my education. Upon reaching adulthood, I was able to obtain a scholarship to university, and upon completion, I entered a position in the City – again through Lord Belving's influence. It was there, yesterday, that I happened to see my mother, in the most unusual manner imaginable.

"I was part of a group of three young men accompanying my supervisor into a meeting. We were standing in the hallway, waiting for our client, when a door to a nearby room opened. As the group inside exited, one of my companions nudged me and nodded toward a woman in black. 'That's the Countess of Houghton,' he said. 'Her husband just died. Worth millions, she is.'

"As this woman stepped into the hallway, speaking to one of our representatives, she glanced my way. The recognition between us was immediate and certain. She was literally rocked back on her heels, and I believe that I was as well. She said something to the men around her, quickly lowered her veil over her face, and set off quickly down the hallway, her companion hurrying to keep up.

"I hurriedly excused myself from my puzzled associates and went after her. I caught up with them in the great hall near the door, calling for her to stop. She turned to me, for just a moment, and I couldn't read her face, although I could see the sparkle of her eyes under the veil. There was so much that I wanted to ask, but I found that my throat was closed. Before I could find the words, she murmured, almost angrily it seemed, 'Leave me be!' and turned away. Her companion, whom I now realize was likely a solicitor, took her elbow and hurriedly directed her toward the door. Before I had sense to follow, she was gone."

"And did you relay this story to your father?" I asked.

Andrew Cole shook his head. "Sadly, he passed two years ago. He had always been a broken man, and gradually he simply seemed to lose interest in the business of living. It was almost a blessing."

"And you never," asked Holmes, "found out any other details about the stolen gold?"

"I did not. I'm convinced of my father's innocence, but he was quite reticent on the matter, and as I said, I always felt that there was more to the story."

"What do you wish from us?" asked Holmes, gesturing in my direction. "Although it might bring you some piece of mind, finding the gold now wouldn't bring your father any comfort, although it might clear his reputation. However, the facts of the matter could end up being as damning as it has always been assumed."

"I want to know the truth. I always have, and this meeting with my mother, however brief, has sharpened that to an urgent degree. I could not sleep last night. But as you say, dredging things up now might make matters worse for all concerned. My mother has apparently made a new and successful life for herself, although I know not how. What if my own clumsy and amateur investigation were to spoil that for her somehow? I thought of you, Mr. Holmes, and realized that you could apply your talents with the skill of a surgeon. Will you look into the matter?"

Holmes was quiet for a moment, his gaze far away, and then he seemed to pull himself back to the present. "I will, Mr. Cole, on the condition that you leave matters in my hands entirely. As you say, there is the possibility that this old business could have fresh implications and most unsatisfactory results."

"Then I shall be satisfied. I'll return to my place of business – here is my card – and will await your report."

With that, hands were shaken, and our young visitor departed. Turning to me, Holmes asked, "Do you have a few hours free, Watson?" I suspect he already knew the answer, and when I replied affirmatively, he responded, "Excellent!" Rubbing his hands, he set about getting ready, and in just a few moments, he was locking the front door behind us while I whistled for the third empty cab to pass by. Soon we were heading toward Whitehall and New Scotland Yard.

The streets weren't crowded, and it wasn't long at all before we were seated in front of our old friend, Inspector Lestrade, explaining our mission. A pained look crossed his face, and he stood up, looking from his window toward the Westminster Pier down below, a location which I shall ever associate as being the initial point of departure for what ended up being a dangerous river chase down the Thames, ending near the Plumstead Marshes.

"Leland Cole," muttered Lestrade, "is a blot upon the Yard's copy-book."

"Would you care to elaborate?" asked Holmes.

The inspector shook his head. "It's distasteful, Holmes. We were just a few years past the scandals, and all of us were working to build respect for our profession. And then Cole goes and murders a pack of robbers and steals the gold."

"Which has yet to be found," I added.

"That's right," said Lestrade. "Which only makes it worse. The entire case is still on the books as unsolved."

"I believe we understand the basic facts – the men were put to sleep, and then killed when they couldn't resist. They had obviously been hiding in that house ever since the theft. Were there any other facts that were not related in the press at the time? Something that the police held back, as you often do?"

Lestrade ran a hand over the lower part of his face, glancing again out of the window. "No, Mr. Holmes, it was very straightforward. The food was analysed, especially when someone asked how three men would have sat there patiently at table and allowed their throats to be cut. We know that they had the gold – they were identified, as you may recall, by an eyewitness during the theft – and there was no coin found with them. Obviously whoever went to the trouble to kill them, silence them, took it, and it hasn't been found since."

"Was there anything that would have made the loot identifiable?" I asked. "Were the coins unusual, for instance?"

"No, Doctor, nothing about them stood out. And there wasn't a flood of them suddenly appearing to indicate that they were being spent. They simply vanished, and have remained that way for nearly a decade."

Holmes frowned. "If there was nothing unusual about the murders – if one can say that the poisoning was normal – then what about the robbery of the gold itself?"

"It occurred two weeks before. It was being loaded into wagons, carried in chests from the basement of Drummonds to be moved to Close Brothers. The transfer was carried out in the evening, in order to minimize interest, in the mistaken belief that not attracting attention to it would make the move more successful. Only later was it determined that the Close Brother's receiving carriage was not manned by their employees, as planned, but rather by the Wards, who had tied up the actual bank employees some hours earlier and left them in an empty room in Cheapside. It was only by accident that a passer-by identified Marcus Ward as one of the men loading the carriage and was able to put us onto their identity. We wasted a lot of time looking for them around their home in Oak Ridge, near Woking. That's how the press named them the; Oak Ridge Gang. However, we had no signs of them until we were notified – by Leland Cole – of the discovery of their bodies a couple of weeks later."

"And there was no other clue? Nothing else about the robbery itself?"

"Nothing, except that we decided that it had to have been planned with inside information, someone at one of the banks, so that the Wards would know how to arrange to take the place of the actual guards in order to receive the money."

"And were there any clues as to who this inside person was?"

"None. All of the employees at each bank passed muster." He frowned, and after a moment added, "Except . . . ."

"Hmm?"

"It's nothing, I'm sure, but there *was* a cleaning woman at the time, at the Close Brothers building, who was unaccounted for after the fact. Simply stopped coming to work in the evenings, and we couldn't trace her. But that probably meant nothing. After all, people like that leave and change jobs all the time."

"No doubt," said Holmes, rising. "Thank you, Inspector. You've provided us with a great deal of help."

Lestrade gave him a canny look. "I trust that you'll let me know where this leads."

"I am always on the side of justice, as you know," replied Holmes. I believe that Lestrade understood the unspoken implications of that statement as well as I.

Outside, Holmes led us west toward Parliament. "I must send a few wires, and then, while we wait for replies, what do you say to a restoration of the inner man?"

I agreed, and we strolled toward a nearby telegraph office, where Holmes composed his messages, and then informed the clerk that we would return in an hour for replies. Then, as if by mutual agreement, we made our way round and about to Northumberland Street, and so into a fine pub of our acquaintance, where we passed the time with a late lunch.

About two o'clock found us back at the telegraph office, where Holmes's replies were waiting. One was from Andrew Cole, stating simply that, during the months leading up to the incident, his father has worked a shift spread over the afternoon and into the late evening, and that his mother hadn't worked at all. The second was from Langdale Pike, that cesspool of societal gossip, indicating that the Countess of Houghton was currently residing in her Mayfair home. There were various other facts about the lady's background in the lengthy message. I confess that as I read through her *vitae*, I couldn't understand how such a woman could have once been Cole's humble mother. Holmes waved Pike's wire in the air. "I think I see a bold venture in our futures, Watson. And as they say, '*Nothing ventured, nothing gained.*'" Hailing a cab, we set out for Bruton Place.

Fifteen minutes later, we stood before a well-kept but discreet multi-storey house. A ring of the bell resulted in the appearance of a man in his fifties, opening the door with a quizzical expression. We presented our cards and were invited inside, to wait and see if the lady of the house was at home.

I knew but little about the Countess, having never heard of her until a few weeks earlier, when it was reported in the press that her much older husband had died of a coronary thrombosis while traveling with her upon the Continent. I knew that we were treading dangerously on bad form by visiting a recent widow in such a manner, but I had long ago learned to swallow discomfort in such situations when in the presence of Sherlock Holmes. He had no patience for such societal contrivances, and as had often proven to be the case, he was correct in his beliefs.

The butler who had initially greeted us showed us into a formal sitting room, and in just a moment, the lady herself entered, accompanied by a silky man in his thirties. Like the Countess, he was dressed in black, and he hovered near her, his hand darting toward her often – not quite touching her, but almost. I wondered if this was the man that Andrew Cole had thought to be her solicitor.

"Gentlemen?" he asked. "What is the meaning of this intrusion? Surely you are aware of the Countess's recent loss. There are better times and ways to pay your respects."

"And you are?" asked Holmes.

"I am Milton Crane, a close friend and advisor to the Countess."

"I see," said Holmes. Turning to the lady, Holmes said, "Madam, do you think it wise to discuss your personal business in front of this gentleman?"

She lifted her veil then and gave a tight smile. She was a handsome woman in her mid-forties, well kept, and still quite lovely. In her younger days, she would have certainly been a beauty indeed. "I have no secrets from Milton," she said. "Won't you be seated?" She gestured toward a grouping of chairs, and – under Milton Crane's disapproving gaze – we all found our places.

"As you wish," said Holmes, "*Mrs. Cole.*"

The lady's eyes widened, clearly surprised, as I was myself. Holmes had apparently decided to cut through the politeness and subterfuge and proceed to the heart of the matter. Milton Crane started to make some sort of squawk, but her raised hand was enough to instantly silence him.

The Countess smiled tightly. "I see that Andrew didn't wait long at all before setting you upon my trail."

Holmes nodded. "Your son…"

"*Son!*" exclaimed Crane. "The Countess has no son!"

"Do be quiet, Milton," she said, without vexation, or really without any emotion whatsoever. "You surely knew that I had a life before I married Eustace."

"But a *son*. Why, I never had any idea. Why wasn't I told?" Another wave of the hand, and he sank and subsided back into a chair, a puzzled look filling his smooth face.

"I was glad to see Andrew looking so well," she said. "I had quite lost track of him. Although to be honest, it was intentional. Once, soon after I had married Eustace, we were invited to Lord Belving's house in Surrey. I knew that Leland and Andrew were living there by then, and I had to feign an illness in order to avoid attending."

Holmes leaned back and crossed his legs. "Your son," he said with a disarming smile, "mentioned that he slept quite deeply, back around the time of your first husband's tribulations."

"First husband?" said Crane.

Her eyes narrowed, her expression wary. "What of it?"

"Oh, nothing, I suppose. Perhaps it's simply a coincidence that he was sleeping so well, at around the same time the three men were drugged with opiates."

"You really aren't making any sense, Mr. Holmes."

"I suppose not," he agreed. "I wonder if anyone at Close Brothers remembers the cleaning woman who suddenly abandoned her post, all those years ago. She worked in the evenings, I believe."

Except for a flaring of her thin nostrils, there was no reaction. Crane was looking back and forth between he lady at his side and Holmes, uncertain as to what was happening. "*Nothing ventured,*" I thought to myself, having almost caught up. However, having caught the ship, I was now struggling to stay on board, in spite of having had the benefit of seeing Langdale Pike's wire.

Turning his head, Holmes asked, "Mr. Crane, when did you meet the Countess?"

"What? Oh, three or four years ago, at Ascot. Since then, our circles have intersected more and more often, and we became . . . better acquainted. Then, when the Count passed away several weeks ago, I was able to, you know, make myself useful."

"Indeed. Fortunately, the Countess, *nee* Mrs. Cole, has indicated that she has no secrets from you, so we can discuss matters in a frank and forthright manner. Do you agree, madam?"

He had pivoted his hawk-like gaze back toward the black-clad lady, who was watching him as a small animal ponders a snake – afraid to move, and afraid to run.

"I really don't know why you're here, Mr. Holmes. What you refer to happened ten years ago." Turning to Crane, she explained, "I was once in much less fortunate circumstances than when you first encountered me, Martin. I was rather common, you see, and married to a *policeman.*"

86

She said it the same as if she'd said *leper*. "He got himself mixed up in a crime – probably not for the first time, since that was in the days of the various police corruption scandals – and I really had no choice but to get away from him."

Crane nodded, apparently looking for any way to excuse her past actions. I interjected, "But your son, madam! Your own child! How could you abandon him as you did, leaving him with a man that you believed to be a criminal?"

She frowned, and her cold façade seemed to crack in the very slightest way. "You don't understand. You cannot. To be trapped in that life – that *slattern* that I was forced to be was not the person that I truly am. I had always known that I belonged in better circumstances…that I could do so much more with my life. Marrying…marrying Leland was a mistake. I didn't think so at the time. I thought that it would make things better, more complete. That it would be a step up. They were always telling me to settle, to accept my place. As if it were my fate!"

She became more agitated as she spoke, and I asked again, "But your child?"

"*Child!*" she snapped. "I never wanted a *child*! Being a mother was simply another part of the role that I had to play, being the wife of a common policeman. I suppose at the time that I believed that it might help. I saw all the other women finding purpose and meaning with their children. It seemed to be a way for them to escape from their lives by having such distractions. But I never understood. I tried, for years and years I tried, but I just couldn't. Andrew only reminded me every day of how the coils of that life were slipping tighter and tighter around my throat!"

Crane was looking at her now with something like the way that one sees a complete stranger. The sudden change in her had shocked him. His fluttering motions toward her, constant up to this point, had ceased as he folded his hands tightly in his lap, as if he were protecting himself.

"And so you went off to the Continent," prompted Holmes.

She nodded. "When Leland had his…troubles, it seemed like a heaven-sent opportunity. I tried to stay with him, to reason with him, after the killings, but he wouldn't have any of it. He could have come with me. We could have even taken Andrew. We could have started over together. But instead, he kept clinging to the idea that we could go on as we had."

"You left them then, and made your way to the Continent. Did you never wonder about them? About the husband and son that you had abandoned?"

"I did. At first." She was trying to give the appearance that none of it had mattered, but emotion was altering her voice, roughening it as she spoke more urgently. "God help me, I wanted to cut the cords, but it wasn't as easy as I thought it would be. But as time passed."

"As time passed," interrupted Holmes, "you accustomed yourself to your new lifestyle, and you met and married the Count, and discovered that you had finally found the life that you'd been missing for all those years."

"Yes!" she hissed. "Yes. I was finally *happy!*"

"Did you know that your first husband, Leland, died two years ago?"

Her eyes widened. "No…No, I didn't. I…I stopped keeping track of them at some point."

"Did you ever actually divorce him?"

Crane was, by this time, leaning forward intently on the edge of his chair.

"I…no, I…that is to say, not officially."

"So your marriage to the Count was bigamous."

No answer.

"Mr. Crane?" snapped Holmes.

"Um, yes?"

"How much was the Count's fortune?"

"Well, it was…that is to say, it is five million pounds."

"Who are his heirs?"

"Why, the Countess."

"No one else?"

"No."

"She was named in the will?"

"I believe so."

"And now that we know that she is *not* his wife, who are the other heirs?"

"Well, there are some estranged children, from a previous marriage."

"Estranged? How so?"

Crane glanced at the Countess…that is to say, Mrs. Cole…with a sour look. "They were close to the Count, until he married the Countess. Um, until he *thought* that he was marrying his current wife." He turned back to Holmes. "Until he married this woman." He swallowed and continued. "Mr. Holmes, I have some association with the legalities of the Estate. Can you prove any of this?"

Holmes fished out Pike's telegram. "Yes." Without handing it to Crane, he turned back to Mrs. Cole, who was now hunched forward, looking decidedly less attractive than she had before, her eyes fixed on the slip of paper. "What would an autopsy reveal, madam, regarding the Count's death?" Glancing my way, he said, "A coronary thrombosis can be *caused*, can it not, Doctor?"

"Yes."

"If such an act were deliberately induced, would it be noticed in an elderly patient?"

"Not necessarily."

Holmes nodded. Turning back to Mrs. Cole and holding up the telegram, he asked, "Was it difficult to establish yourself when you first arrived in Nice, ten years ago?"

"What?" she asked, clearly off balance and trying to change directions from her thoughts about the Count's death. "What?"

"Ten years ago. When you arrived in Nice with the stolen gold. Your history is well established afterwards, but nothing before. You appeared out of nowhere, it seems, wealthy, but with a certain, shall we say, *crudity* unbefitting a lady accustomed to old money. However, you were a quick learner, and apparently spent your funds wisely in terms of both clothing and choosing where to appear. It wasn't long before you had made the Count's acquaintance, was it?"

She shook her head, as if something were buzzing around her ears. "Mr. Crane," asked Holmes. "How did the Count's first wife die?"

"Why, she fell from one of the cliffs during a nighttime walk."

Glancing at the wire, Holmes said, "And that would have been in the spring of 1881, I believe."

A look of enlightenment and shock passed across Crane's face. "I think that's right."

Back to Mrs. Cole: "Just a few months after your arrival in Nice, and just a few months *before* your quick marriage to the Count."

She shook her head. It was appalling to see how quickly the lady had fallen from the confident creature that had first walked into the room.

"I doubt if you've changed all that much in ten years – you've likely worked to preserve yourself. So I have to ask," said Holmes, "isn't it likely that the staff at Close Brothers will recall when you worked there as a cleaning lady, while your husband was at work, and when your poor son was at home, drugged and sleeping deeply from the same opiates that you would later use in the Wards' food?"

I had seen Holmes do this before – battering someone with facts from so many different directions, the same way that he kept a bare-knuckle opponent off balance by gracefully dancing from side-to-side, throwing punches from one direction and then the other, seemingly at random, but in fact scientifically calculated to crumble any resistance.

"No," said the lady. "No, they wouldn't know me. I changed my appearance."

"Good," said Holmes. "No need to follow that up, then." She looked up, almost happy that he was agreeing with her, too confused now to realize what was happening. "We progress. And the Wards? How did you become involved with their scheme?"

"I knew Marcus, when I was a girl. We grew up together. There was some understanding that we would marry, but I couldn't...I just couldn't do that. I settled for Leland, thinking that path would be a better way. I didn't see Marcus for years, but then I ran into him one day in the street. We began to talk, and we kept meeting. It wasn't anything to me, just a way to avoid the terrible monotony, but he believed it was becoming something more.

"He told me about the gold. He had heard of it from one of his friends. He and his two sons from his earlier marriage were prepared to try and steal it, but they needed to know when it would be moved. He helped me get a job with the Close Brothers. I would slip some of the powder into Andrew's food...Marcus gave it to me for just that reason – after Leland went to work, and while the boy ...while my son slept, I would clean the offices and read their papers. They never worried about putting them away or covering them up...they never paid any attention to us at all."

"And then the Wards stole the gold."

"That's right. And Marcus wanted me to run away with him. But that would have been trading just one kind of despair for another."

"And what happened the night of the murder?"

Apparently, she couldn't stop herself now. Perhaps the secrets had cried out too long for confession. "I had decided what I needed to do. To get the money. But I didn't know that Leland was scheduled to get off from work early that night. He arrived in our street and saw me leaving. Without telling me, he followed. I went to where Marcus and the others were hiding and...and poisoned their food. I started to just take the gold then and disappear, but I realized that I would never be able to stop looking over my shoulder. So... so I did it. I killed them."

Crane stood up then and took a step back, knocking into his chair. Mrs. Cole didn't notice.

"I took the gold and left. It was heavy, but I could just carry it in two leather cases. I took it home and buried it in an abandoned shed near where we lived, so it wouldn't be found. Leland, who had seen me go into the hiding place, let me go without revealing himself, and then went inside to see why I had been there. I had shut the door behind me when I left...he only said that he had found it open as a reason for him to enter. He discovered the bodies inside. He recognized the Wards, and he told me later that he put together the fact that I was the missing cleaning lady. Being a good policeman, he couldn't just walk away. He sounded the alarm, not realizing that he was implicating himself, as he couldn't satisfactorily explain why he was in that neighbourhood.

"After several days of not speaking about it, his will broke. He confronted me, and I confessed. I tried to get him to go away with me...I really did. I was willing to include him and the child in my new life, but he wouldn't have any of it. As the days went on, he fell more and more under suspicion, but of course he couldn't give me up. The anger between us grew, and finally I couldn't stand it any longer. I retrieved the coins and left them. And he...he kept my secret all these years. And now...now you tell me that he's dead?"

Finally, at this point she seemed to run down, and a single tear tracked along her cheek. "Watson," said Holmes softly. "Summon Lestrade."

Later, we were back in Baker Street, and I asked to see Langdale Pike's telegram once again. It was all there – the raw facts that had allowed Holmes to see the invisible threads that connected them. "She had appeared out of nowhere in France at about the same that Mrs. Cole had disappeared. This only confirmed that the woman Andrew Cole saw yesterday, a Countess, as in fact his humble mother. When this woman arrived in Nice ten years ago, she was clearly wealthy. Where had the money come from to finance this life? Pike, though curious, of course had no knowledge about that aspect, but the connection is obvious to us, who can see both sides. We know that the woman who surfaced in France was also married to a policeman who was accused of stealing a fortune in gold which had never been recovered. Lestrade's fortuitous mention of a missing cleaning woman, along with Andrew's offhand reference to sleeping deeply at around the same time that men died because they were given opiates, was enough to cause the idea to coalesce in my mind. The only real challenge was to pick at different threads throughout her whole construct until enough of them weakened and it all came apart, letting her fall through."

At that moment, the bell rang, and Holmes went downstairs to let in Andrew Cole, recently summoned. After Holmes brought him up, the young man resumed the seat that had held him that morning. Trying to sound jovial, he asked, "News already? That was fast, gentlemen." Then, seeing our rather grim expressions, his wan smile dropped, and he said flatly, "Tell me."

And Holmes did, laying it out linearly and simply. When he was done, the young man thought for a moment and then stood. "Thank you, Mr. Holmes. Dr. Watson," he said simply. "I don't know what to think, really. She ceased to be my mother a long time ago, but I am glad to know the truth about my poor father, who kept her secret to the end. He must have loved her all the way."

"Yes," I murmured.

"Inspector Lestrade will be in touch," said Holmes. "Your father did have knowledge that he held back about a crime, but there were . . . extenuating and understandable circumstances. I believe that he would like to discuss it with you."

"Certainly. You can tell him where to find me. And please send your bill to the same location. I believe that I gave you my card?"

Holmes nodded and stood. I followed. We each shook Andrew Cole's hand, and the young man passed out of our lives and back into that throng of four millions all jostling each other within the space of a few miles. We were destined to meet him again, but that is another tale.

Smoking quietly, we passed a solemn hour until it was time for me to arise and walk back to Paddington. Holmes, deep in his own meditations, looked up and gave a nod, which I returned. Then, letting myself out, I returned to my wife, very fortunate indeed in knowing that I had the truest treasure of them all.

David Marcum's Top Ten:

1. The Adventure of The Speckled Band
2. The Hound of the Baskervilles
3. The Adventure of The Final Problem
4. The Adventure of The Empty House
5. The Adventure of The Norwood Builder
6. The Adventure of The Bruce-Partington Plans
7. The Adventure of The Red-Headed League
8. The Adventure of The Copper Beeches
9. The Adventure of The Musgrave Ritual
10. The Adventure of The Second Stain

'What is it, Holmes?'
'It's a hat stand, Watson.'

Pantoum in B Minor... Jennifer Met

These moments he's lost
in a hungry catgut whining—him awake—
a lark—fiddling his lap to
something like a dream

in a hungry cat's gut—whining him awake—
for one who never sleeps,
something like a dream
is all he has.

For one who never sleeps
is here—solidly—sawing his own REM.
Is all he has
just a memory of opium? Is oblivion real?

And is here, solidly sawing his own REM
a lark? Fiddling his lap, too,
just a memory of opium's oblivion, really, and
those moments he's lost.

Jennifer Met's Top Ten:

1. The Adventure of the Speckled Band
2. The Hound of the Baskervilles
3. The Adventure of the Copper Beeches
4. The Adventure of the Dancing Men
5. The Adventure of the Red-Headed League
6. The Man with the Twisted Lip
7. A Study in Scarlet
8. The Adventure of the Dying Detective
9. A Scandal in Bohemia
10. The Adventure of the Greek Interpreter

Poetic (In)Justice...set by Mark Mower

Help Sherlock Holmes to solve the six murder mystery Haiku poems below. All the clues you need to identify the name of the killer are contained within each verse:

Verse 1
Gardener dead – was it
Tinker, tailor, soldier, spy?
Warm blood on red soil.

Verse 2
Bob poisoned by girl.
Found mainly on open moor,
Partly in error.

Verse 3
Boy shot in death verse.
Killer named in other ode.
Who pulled the trigger?

Verse 4
Gunman fired then hid.
Dying man drew attention
to slayer within.

Verse 5
Man killed in bonfire.
Wife suspected, and clue found
in pile of red ash.

The Mystery of the Disappearing Duster...S F Bennett

I have noted elsewhere in these chronicles that Mrs Hudson, the landlady of Mr Sherlock Holmes, and on occasion mine, was a most tolerant woman. That she was also long-suffering is without question; that she had a great deal of respect for her remarkable lodger – a sentiment I believe was mutual – too is beyond doubt.

It is fair to say that the worse of his faults she overlooked where a less forgiving person might not. Despite her grumbles when the chemical smells from the first-floor rooms became unbearable or when the midnight concerts kept her from her sleep, I fancy she harboured a certain fondness for her celebrated tenant, both for the lustre he added to her address and in her self-appointed role as guardian of the threshold, a responsibility she defended most jealously. Any client wishing to see Holmes had first to win the approval of Mrs Hudson, and anyone foolhardy enough to think to side-step the good lady was briskly reminded that here was not a woman who brooked discourteous behaviour lightly.

They had forged an understanding, Holmes and Mrs Hudson, one marked by wary regard on both sides and few upsets. Generally speaking, their relationship was harmonious, but appearances can be deceptive. An unspoken war bubbled beneath the otherwise placid surface of life at 221b, and at its heart lay the question of dust.

Quite simply, Mrs Hudson saw it as the bane of her life. Her own domain she endeavoured to keep as free of city grime as was humanly possible. To her credit, I had never known a time when the banisters did not bear that brilliant gleam produced by endless polishing. The front step was always washed down before the postman arrived and visitors were greeted by the sight of a spotlessly clean mat in the hall. What others might see as a virtue, however, Holmes always contended was a nuisance.

I am not the tidiest man in the world, but I do have my limits. I feel that when one is able to inscribe one's name in the dust on the bookcase, then a spring clean of some description is most definitely in order. Not considering myself an expert on such things, I also contend that such important work is also better undertaken by others, in my case by the maid under the careful supervision of my wife.

Holmes, however, takes a different view. He has always maintained that dust, like mud, is most instructive. Dust on a man's hat means his wife has ceased to love him. Ingrained dust on the shoes, so he says, tells of a careless disposition produced by some malign influence. The type of dust, the smell of dust, even the colour of it is for him a fascination that quite escapes me. When he acquired a microscope, he began to study it in even greater detail and claimed he was going to write a monograph on the subject. I could only imagine what his publishers thought of that.

For myself, I tend to dismiss it as nothing more than a threat to the cleanliness of one's cuffs. I take a purely practical view of the matter. When I see dust, I tend to brush it away – or if I am not being watched, I sweep it under the carpet. I certainly do not wallow in it, as Holmes seems to do. This is where he and Mrs Hudson do not see eye to eye.

The state of his rooms is her *bête noire*. She covets the dust on his desk as one might the rarest jewel. Many times have I caught her, gazing longingly at his closed door, duster in hand. I imagine she dreams of the wonders she could work if only he would permit her the most perfunctory of cleans. That he does not only causes her resentment to simmer all the more.

By so doing, he has encouraged underhand tactics on her part, worthy of the most formidable of foes. In this, I must admit to having been a willing conspirator. Excessive dust affects my sinuses and Holmes tends to grumble unkind things if my visits are marked by constant sneezing. Between us, Mrs Hudson and I have conspired to make a tidier man of him.

Clandestine sorties take place when he leaves the house, it being my task to keep him away long enough for Mrs Hudson to work her magic. She never moves anything and is careful not to disturb his work, but the fresh smell of polish always betrays her presence. Holmes says nothing, although I know these surreptitious cleaning sprees of hers deeply irritates him.

He retaliates by throwing his tobacco on the floor, usually when she is collecting the breakfast things and can observe quite clearly what he is doing, and leaving the window open when the chimney sweep is at work to ensure that the soot is spread far and wide. Certainly a man has a right to his dust, but this behaviour smacks of childish petulance.

This is the game they play, Holmes and his landlady, like two warring generals, neither willing to back down and always looking to gain advantage over the other. The matter has never been addressed outright; instead this tacit war continues, as bitter as any taken to the field of battle.

So it was that when we returned from a brief stay in Cornwall in the summer of 1889, I had every expectation of finding that Mrs Hudson had taken the opportunity of Holmes's absence to effect a thorough clean of the house. He was in good humour, having successfully concluded the shocking business of the Nude Cyclist of the Mandervilles, a retelling of which would, I fear, be neither edifying nor advisable for readers of a nervous disposition.

All the way home he had talked volubly and at length about a quick succession of topics – on the references to Humanism in the music of Josquin, medieval astrology, the philosophy of Spinoza and the forthcoming Paris Exhibition. I struggled to keep pace with his enthusiasm and finally gave up the attempt, revelling instead in his bright humour that I knew from experience would evaporate once he caught the whiff of beeswax polish and saw a shine on the floorboards.

I was braced for confrontation as our cab came to a halt outside the door. Instead I found Mrs Hudson in a state of great agitation.

"Oh, Mr Holmes," she cried, hurrying out to meet us before we had a chance to set foot inside. "There have been burglars here in your absence, sir. We have been robbed and my poor home invaded!"

Whilst Holmes accepted this news with equanimity, I was deeply concerned.

"What was taken?" I asked. "Did they go upstairs?"

"I'm not sure," said she. "It all happened so fast, sir. One minute I was seeing Mr Holmes off to the station to meet you, Doctor, and the next..." Her bottom lip trembled. "I didn't turn my back for more than half a minute, I'm sure of it."

"That's all these criminals need, Mrs Hudson," I reassured her. "It's no fault of yours, I'm sure. Isn't that right, Holmes?"

"They used to call them 'dead lurkers'," said he, absently.

"What?"

"Opportunist thieves who stole coats and umbrellas from passages when doors were left open. That was the 'official' term for them some years back." His eyes had taken on that languid look that told me his thoughts were disengaged from the matter at hand. "I've often wondered," he went on, "whether such people were exclusive in their 'trade'. What if one tired of stealing umbrellas and took to stealing clothes from washing lines instead? Would the other 'snow gatherers' as they were called object to the competition? Could one be both at the same time?"

"Is this entirely relevant?" I protested. "Mrs Hudson has had a most distressing experience."

"That I do not deny, although I am bound to say it was most careless of you, Mrs Hudson, to leave the door unattended. And may I say, most unlike you."

"I'm thoroughly ashamed of myself," said the poor woman, bitterly wringing her hands, "and I don't mind admitting it. I've never had so much as bootlace stolen from my hall before."

"What did they take?" I asked.

"That's the thing of it, Doctor. They took my best feather duster and the half tin of Brightwell's Floor Polish. I don't understand it at all."

"Pointless," I agreed. "They could make little profit from your duster, Mrs Hudson."

"My best duster, sir. I've had that same one for thirty-six years. A faithful friend that's been, and only cost me a few pennies in having to replace the handle and the feathers."

"How then can it be the same duster?" Holmes queried. "By your own admission, if both handle and feathers are replacements—"

"Most curious," I said, interrupting him before he confused the issue further. "What do you make of it, Holmes? Why would thieves steal such trivial items?"

Perhaps they needed a new handle for their own duster?"

I shot him a look of reproof. "Sounds like a diversionary tactic to me. I think we should check upstairs, in case there was an ulterior motive to this theft. It could be that they were attempting to gain access to your files."

Mrs Hudson snorted. "It would take them longer than a minute to find what they were looking for up there."

Upstairs, my worst fears were realised. Papers were strewn across the floor, every drawer was pulled open, and books taken from the shelves had been flung around in wild abandon.

"Dear heavens!" I exclaimed. "You've been burgled."

"Don't be absurd, Watson," said my companion, placing his hat, cane and bag on the table. "This is exactly how I left it. Good, I see that nothing has been disturbed."

Stepping deftly across the litter, he proceeded to locate and charge his pipe, and then, having swept an assortment of newspaper cuttings from his fireside chair, settled down with a sigh of satisfaction. His behaviour puzzled me and I was most exasperated that he should dismiss what to me seemed a most serious matter so lightly.

"Aren't you in the least concerned?" I asked.

He shook his head.

"Thieves do not steal items of little value unless they have a good reason."

"Then what do you suggest, Watson? That we call upon the massed ranks of the Metropolitan Police and send them out in search of a purloined duster? I dare say they would find that most amusing at Scotland Yard."

"How many times have you said in the past that the most trifling incident may have the most sinister of implications?"

"I stand by that claim."

"Then why are you dismissing this theft out of hand?"

He gazed at me enquiringly through blue-grey smoke rings as they chased each other to the ceiling. I gathered that he wished me to make up my own mind about the matter, which could only mean that he had himself arrived at a logical answer.

"You know what occurred here, don't you?" I said.

"Quite so."

"Are you going to share this information with me?"

He smiled and closed his eyes. "I had hoped you would arrive at your own conclusion. You know my methods."

"Applying them, however, is another matter. Very well. Whoever stole these items had a good reason for doing so."

"Oh, the very best."

"And you would agree that the financial gain from dusters and floor polish is very little. Therefore the motive must be a personal one, calculated to disturb Mrs Hudson and inconvenience her. Ah, I have it! Mrs James, two doors along, is the culprit. She never forgave Mrs Hudson for taking in that ginger kitten. She always said that cat ate her canary."

If I spoke with some authority, it was because I was pleased with what seemed to me a satisfactory explanation. Holmes, however, slowly opened his eyes and favoured me with a look of pity.

"My dear fellow, as amusing as it is listening to you casting Mrs James in the role of villain, I feel it is my duty to remind you that the lady in question is over eighty and walks with the aid of two sticks. Is this the opportunist thief who dashed in when Mrs Hudson's back was turned but for a minute? No, Watson, it will not do."

I was a little offended by this curt dismissal of my efforts. "She has her nephew staying with her at present."

"This is the same nephew who not a month ago asked you to keep an eye on his aunt because he thought she was going peculiar? You think he would accede to her wishes in this matter?"

"Yes, if he thought to humour her."

Holmes rose with a sigh and knocked the spent ash from his pipe into the grate. "Watson, I have done you an injustice. In watering the arid desert of your imagination, I have encouraged excessive bloom. I am bound to tell you that you have erred by confusing the issue with talk of elderly ladies, nephews and dead canaries. Simplify, simplify, to remind you of Thoreau's exhortation."

"An opportunist thief then?"

He shook his head sharply. "You assume that a theft has taken place."

"You mean to say that Mrs Hudson has simply misplaced her duster and polish?"

"Or it has been borrowed."

"Borrowed by whom?"

"By one of the principal players in this petty drama."

I gave his words due consideration and a startling thought occurred to me. "Holmes, surely you didn't!"

He wandered across to the table and extracted from his bag a moth-eaten feathered item that had once been its owner's pride and joy. "I am afraid I did," said he, adding the missing tin of polish to the collection of incriminating evidence. "I happened to see these items as I was leaving and the temptation was too great. I know what transpires here in my absence. I am also fully aware that you, who call yourself my friend, happily collude with my landlady against me."

"I do not," I protested.

"Do not attempt to deny it. You should be thoroughly ashamed of yourself."

"Well, what if I do? Look at the state of this place. However do you find anything in this confusion?"

"What you call confusion I call organisation. I know exactly where everything is. And that dust, which you both find most objectionable, is for me a somewhat primitive attempt at security. I have no doubt that there are several prominent people in London at this very moment who would dearly wish to gain access to my files. The day I find the dust in my rooms disturbed by hands other than my own, then I shall know that I have cause to worry. That is why I cannot allow Mrs Hudson a free rein in here."

"But leaving her to think she had been robbed. Holmes, that is most ungallant of you."

"I am not so unchivalrous an opponent. I fully intend to return this to her, albeit indirectly."

"You will return it to her now with a full apology and put her mind at rest." I opened the door and called down to her. "Mrs Hudson, would you mind coming up here for a moment?"

Holmes grabbed me by the arm and hauled me back. "Have you lost your senses? An apology – why it is tantamount to surrender! I shall never know a moment's peace if I allow you to grant Mrs Hudson this unreasonable hold over me. You forget, the opening salvo in this conflict was not mine. As for Mrs Hudson's peace of mind, her good sense should have told her that thieves do not waste their time on trivial items such as these."

"Very well. I shall tell her I found the lost items upstairs where she had left them."

"My dear fellow, despite your experience of matrimony, you are still woefully ignorant of the minds of women. Mrs Hudson will not for one moment believe this tale you intend to weave. She will know."

"Perhaps so, but my way allows you both to retain face. And then you will have to come to an understanding about this situation. This cannot continue."

Mrs Hudson chose that moment to appear. Her eye fell upon the missing articles in an instant and, throughout my brief invention of how I found them in my former room upstairs, I could not fail to notice that her gaze was fixed accusingly on Holmes.

"Well, I've got them back," said she, her expression, if not her tone, suggesting that she was thoroughly unconvinced by my tale, "so we'll say no more about it, although it seems a mighty strange thing to me how they could have got upstairs,

Doctor, when I'm sure I had them in my little basket by the front door."

"You must have been mistaken," said Holmes, rubbing his hands as if pleased to be free of the matter. "You have your feather duster, Mrs Hudson, I have another case that demands my attention and Watson must be getting home to his wife. All's well that ends well. What a very satisfactory day."

I cleared my throat. Holmes's face fell. He may have avoided the apology, but I was determined to have this resolved one way or another.

"Mrs Hudson," said he in the slow measured tones of a condemned man facing his executioner, "it has been brought to my attention that you have been somewhat slack in your housekeeping regarding the state of this room."

"Slack, sir? If I have, it is because you will not allow me access, and in my own house, mark you!"

At least Holmes had the decency to look a little abashed. "Yes, I fear I have been busy of late. The disturbance would have been... difficult. All the same, I feel that a flick round the shelves with that duster of yours would not go amiss. I believe I could tolerate the occasional intrusion. Oh, say, once a year."

"Is that what you say?" said she, her mouth pursed into a wrinkle of displeasure. "The dust will be a foot high if we leave it that long. No, sir, it will have to be every week or not at all. Those are my terms."

"Mrs Hudson, that is—"

I gave a warning cough to remind him of his obligations.

"Quite acceptable," he capitulated with an annoyed glance in my direction.

"I'm glad to hear it, Mr Holmes," said she. "You'll soon see the benefit, sir. And you needn't worry, I won't touch any of your things... or hide them, unlike some people I could mention." Holmes said nothing, although her barb had reached its target.

"Well, there's so much to do, I'm sure I don't know where to begin," said she with relish. "Why don't you make a start, Mr Holmes by picking up all your papers? I wouldn't want to be accused of disturbing anything."

She left, muttering to herself about soap and wash clothes. Holmes gazed at the assorted litter around him and, with a sigh of resignation, began to clear a pathway through the debris with his foot.

"You do realise," said he when I joined him on all fours to help gather up the mess, "that my system of security has been compromised by this absurd weekly ritual to which I have been forced to submit. I blame you for this, Watson."

"Which would you prefer: a little inconvenience now or a great deal later when you have to find new lodgings?"

"It is a sad thing when a man is forced to choose between the state of his shelves and his continued residence at his favoured address. This day has witnessed the crumbling of the last great male bastion – a man's right to his dust!"

"Holmes, you exaggerate."

"Do I? No, I fear it is a slippery slope all the way from here to domesticity. This is only the beginning. Mark my words, next there will be talk of 'little jobs to do around the house', closely followed by 'if you aren't doing anything, Mr Holmes, perhaps you could get those curtains down'. You see before you a doomed man at the mercy of what promises to be 'cruel and unusual punishments'."

I laughed at his words. "Do you mean to tell me that you need rescuing?"

"Very much so. What do you suggest?"

"Lunch followed by a concert?"

"Do you have the time? Have I not kept you from your home for long enough?

"I'm sure Mary will understand when I tell her it is a mission of mercy."

"There is no cause worthier," said Holmes, taking up a sheaf of papers which he then secreted beneath the cushion of the sofa. "Well, if one's domestic routine is to be upset, it is best done on a full stomach. After all, does not the condemned man get to eat a hearty supper?"

As we were about to leave, Mrs Hudson entered, bearing a bucket and mop.

"Oh, are you going out, sir?" said she. "I had hoped if you were staying, you could get those curtains down for me."

Holmes shot me a conspiratorial smile. "Alas, but I fear I must forgo that particular avenue of pleasure. I'm afraid that less noble duties bear upon us today, Mrs Hudson, which I expect will keep us away for most of the afternoon, by which time I trust you will be finished."

"I'm not sure about that, Mr Holmes. There's enough work here for two hands, let alone one."

"You do not give yourself enough credit. Why, you have worked wonders in the past with less time than this."

"Put like that, sir, I'll do my best."

"Of course you will. Come, Watson, let us help this dear lady in her endeavours by removing ourselves from the premises and thus by our absence speed her labours to completion. Good day, Mrs Hudson. As for the task that lies ahead, I wish you well of it, but I fear to stay would be more than I can bear. Parting, even from one's carefully cultivated dust, truly is such sweet sorrow."

S F Bennett's Top Ten

1. Silver Blaze
2. The Adventure of the Dying Detective
3. The Adventure of the Greek Interpreter
4. The Adventure of the Empty House
5. The Adventure of the Speckled Band
6. The Adventure of the Six Napoleons
7. The Adventure of the Blue Carbuncle
8. The Adventure of the Devil's Foot
9. The Adventure of the Musgrave Ritual
10. The Adventure of the Final Problem

'What is it, Holmes?'

'It's a shop window, Watson.'

Terror of the Green Man...Robert Perret

The warming light of morning was creeping across the floor of 221B Baker Street. Holmes was intently focused on the pruning of his miniature tree, a curiosity he had picked up in Japan during The Adventure of the Blushing Geisha. I, for my part, sat by the window taking in my newspaper and the people strolling by outside. It being spring, the ladies were sporting the newest fashions and adorning themselves with fresh flowers. The good cheer brought about by warm weather was obviously widespread, for Holmes and I had no cases at present with which to occupy ourselves. Thus I was casting about for something to keep Holmes' mind occupied.

"Fascinating!" I said. Holmes did not stir from his gardening. "Do you remember those seeds that were found last year at that Druid campground?"

"Of course. Brynnmoth Henge. Finding seeds ensconced in a bag in the peat that were still viable was a real coup for the botanical world. Those scientists will have the rare chance to observe living specimens from thousands of years ago."

"Just so. And now so shall we."

Holmes finally looked up from his project. "We shall?"

"The Royal Botanical Society is displaying one of the plants that grew from the seeds. It is an invitation-only lecture happening tonight."

"Have we an invitation?"

"I daresay it is but a matter of calling the Society and notifying them that the great Sherlock Holmes would like to attend."

"I prefer not to trade on my name like that."

"Pshaw. I've seen you wield your name like the master key to the city of London. For once it is for your edification rather than for criminal inquiry."

"I suppose a little fresh air would not go amiss."

As I suspected, the Royal Botanical Society was all too eager to invite the famous Detective, and that evening Holmes and I found ourselves taking our seats in the Great Hall of that venerable institution. The audience was seated in a circle around the middle of the room, where a column of curtains dangled to hide the fantastic plant in question. I had expected our arrival to generate some interest, these tweedy sorts were always tantalized by the salacious side of our business, but the room was positively buzzing. All around us genteel people dressed in fine suits and gowns whispered behind their hands and shot furtive looks in our direction.

"Quite a bit of excitement for the unveiling of a plant," Holmes observed.

A nervous looking man of forty years or so approached us. "Mr. Holmes and Dr. Watson I presume?"

"Well met, sir," I said, his hand feeling brittle in my grasp. "And who might you be?"

"My name is Professor Simon Surell. I assisted Professor Ven Dreisling with the *druidae triumphum*, the plant we were to reveal tonight."

"Assisted?"

"I'm afraid Professor Ven Dreisling…" Surell looked at us in great anticipation.

"I see," Holmes rose to full attention. "I take it Professor Ven Dreisling is no longer with us."

"No, sir, he was, well, I suppose murder is the word."

"Why would murder not be the word? What makes you hesitate?"

"If you and Doctor Watson would accompany me?" We took to our feet and followed Surell towards the centre of the room.

"As I recall, Professor Ven Dreisling was a venerable, but aged scholar." I said. "Is it possible that the excitement of this great achievement so late in his career was simply too much?

114

Perhaps a heart attack or embolism. Either could produce symptoms that might appear as poisoning, especially to a botanically focused mind."

"Oh, I'm not worried that he might have been poisoned. In fact I have no doubt about the nature of his death at all."

"I don't understand," said Holmes. "If you are so sure about the nature of his death why do you hesitate to label it murder?"

"Murder is committed by a man. Could a man do this?" Surell threw back one of the curtains and inside we saw a tree dripping with viscera. It dangled from the branches and there was blood coating the inside of the curtains. A mangled corpse lay at the foot of a potted apple tree. Even with my medical training and military experience I felt a brief swoon pull at my knees. Holmes entered the curtained antechamber, careful not to step on the mess below.

"I take your point," Holmes said, bringing a kerchief to his face. "Besides the killing, can you tell me what else I am looking at?"

"I'm sorry, sir?"

"I presume this blackthorn tree is not the vaunted plant specimen of yore?"

"No, sir. This is a garden variety *prunus spinosa.*"

"This is the tree you meant to unveil this evening?"

"Yes, well, no."

"Which is it?"

"If you look over here, through the... matter, you can see where a limb has been torn from the tree. That limb was a sapling grown from the ancient seed, which we had spliced onto the blackthorn tree as a sort of nurse plant."

"So someone killed Professor Ven Dreisling in order to steal this branch?"

"But it looks like they wrenched the branch right off the tree."

"That does appear to be the case. Why do you peer at me incredulously?"

"Have you ever tried to wrench a branch from a tree, Mr. Holmes? It is hard enough to break a twig, never mind this."

"As impressive a trick as that may be, lying on the ground there we already see a greater feat of strength. Any assailant who could tear a man limb from limb could surely do the same of a tree."

"But, why Holmes?" I stammered.

"The motive we can only speculate at this point. Perhaps simple greed. Perhaps a rival researcher. Perhaps a religious fanatic of one stripe or another who wanted to save or destroy the ancient plant. That remains to be seen. The timing, however, I wager is in response to opportunity."

"Sir?"

"I imagine the seeds and their seedlings are well guarded?"

"Of course! We hold the seeds here in the Royal Society vault. The saplings are locked up in the professor's laboratory."

"Carefully controlled access. Someone saw this as their best opportunity."

Holmes produced his famous magnifying glass and began to examine the area in detail, hunched over and prowling like a hound on the scent. Surell fidgeted uncomfortably and I gave him a reassuring nod. After a few minutes Holmes turned back to address us.

"You've no need of a detective, Professor Surell."

"How can that be, Mr. Holmes?"

"As Watson has often heard me say, the most fantastical cases are the easiest to solve. Observe these prints." Holmes gestured at the bloodied ground.

"What prints?"

"I agree with the professor, Holmes. I fancy myself a bit of a print expert after our many cases together but I don't see even the suggestion of one here."

"That is because you are looking for footprints, a first order mistake."

"Now, Holmes, you are always looking for footprints, at practically every crime scene!"

"To the contrary, a first step in my process is to observe the ground for whatever may be there."

"Which, in this case, is footprints, or so you claim."

"Very much so."

"Yet you also claim that I am unable to see the very same footprints because I am looking for them?"

"Precisely, Watson. Now you have it."

"You are not making any sense, Holmes. Perhaps the air in here is too close. Let's step outside and clear our heads."

"What does a footprint look like?"

"Goodness, Holmes! Sit down. Professor Surell, would you fetch Mr. Holmes a glass of water?"

"Right away, Dr. Watson!"

"Stay, professor. Humour me, Watson. What does a footprint look like?"

"Well, I would expect something about this big," I gestured with my hands, "with a gentle curve to the outside and a pronounced curve on the inside. Some sort of circle or semicircle at the heel. A bare foot would of course show toes…"

"Very good, Doctor. Because of your expectations of what a foot should look like you are blind to the prints in this room."

"What! Where?"

"There, there, and there on out of the curtains and no doubt out of the building altogether."

"Those large spots? Surely the perpetrator was lugging a bag with his ill-gotten tree limb or something."

"Large, indeed. I suspected, of course, that any person strong enough to commit these crimes would also be unusually large."

"If those are footprints they belong not to a man but to a giant!"

"Assuming man-like proportions I would estimate over twelve feet tall."

"Amazing!" cried Surell. "How would a man like that enter the Society without notice?"

"Thieves always find a way. A door carelessly propped open, a window not properly latched. When was this presentation announced?"

"At last month's meeting."

117

"A month to examine the premises for weak points. I'd wager he has been in the basement, or attic, for at least a few days, waiting for the stars to align. That's what I would do. Finally, the moment of truth. The tree was in a public area and guarded only by one man. The thief struck. Literally, by the way. Look at the leaves and twigs embedded in the blood. Ven Dreisling was beaten with a branch before he was dismembered."

"All of this seems unnecessarily gruesome."

"A brutish crime, I would say. But a brute was needed to carry off the tree."

Professor Surell now looked at some of the vegetable matter embedded in the blood of his old mentor, with the intellectual detachment natural to scientists of all disciplines. "These leaves, are from the *druidae triumphum*, the ancient plant!"

"The thief beat the professor with the very branch he was stealing?"

"The unthinking instinct of a trapped beast I imagine. In any event the police are looking for a twelve foot tall man soaked in blood and carrying a branch. There is not much more that deduction can tell them. My condolences on the loss of your colleague, Professor. Watson, perhaps it is not too late to find some other amusement as long as we are dressed and about." Holmes spun on his heel and swept through the hanging curtains. I gave an apologetic tip of the hat to Surell and followed.

The next morning I was awakened by shouting out in the street. I opened my window and called down.

"What's this racket all about, then?"

"City Park, guv!" replied a grubby newsboy. "It's grown into a thick, dark forest right out of a grim fairy tale, sir!"

"Nonsense!" I said before slamming my window shut. But the din continued outside. Begrudgingly I dressed and entered the parlour. There was Mrs. Hudson fretting over the newspaper.

"Oh, Dr. Watson! Have you heard? It's terrible!" There on the front page was the title "City Park Grows in the Dark!"

"There, there, Mrs. Hudson. It must be an exaggeration."

"The papers don't think so, and neither does my friend, Millie. She walks right by the park to get to the greengrocer and she saw it with her own eyes."

"We'll all go to the park after breakfast to see for ourselves." I patted her trembling hands.

"We'll do no such thing." Holmes appeared from his bedroom. "I'll not waste a moment of my time on this fantastical nonsense. A handful of manicured trees does not become a deep, dark forest overnight. Impossible!"

"It seems I remember you saying something about the impossible, Mr. Holmes." Mrs. Hudson sniffled into her handkerchief. "And also something about making up your mind without evidence in hand."

"I also remember saying something about two eggs and a rasher of ham for breakfast, if you please!" Holmes seized the paper and held it up to end the conversation. Mrs. Hudson pulled a face as she rose to make Holmes's breakfast. I was glad my eggs were already on my plate. I hesitate to eat anything from an angry cook.

"Take heart, Mrs. Hudson." I offered. "The two of us shall go then."

There was no change in the muttering coming from the kitchen.

Before Mrs. Hudson could return there was a knocking at the door. Already feeling the tension in the flat I announced that I would answer it. Outside stood a steely-eyed Inspector Gregson. I showed him up to the parlour.

"Don't tell me you are unable to find a literal giant running around London," Holmes said before exhaling a plume of tobacco smoke. Gregson ground his hat around in his hands.

"I am here on an entirely different matter."

"Keeping you out of the way of important cases, are they? Wise precaution."

"I'll have you know that no one has seen your supposed giant and that there is even odds down at the station that you have finally gone quite mad."

"If you don't like my answers then why are you here asking me questions?"

"I am here under orders, to which I objected, by the way."

"Duly noted."

"The Captain noted them too, for all the good that's done me. We have a missing wife, Mrs. Haddy Donalson, wife of Michael Donalson. Last seen visiting a friend in South London. A train porter was the last known person to see her. He confirmed seating her in a shared compartment, after which he never saw her leave. Mrs. Donalson, as well as the other two people in the compartment, were nowhere to be found when the train arrived in central London."

"Yet you are not looking for these other two?"

"No one has reported them missing, so we must consider them suspects, of course. Unfortunately it was not until late last night that Mrs. Donalson was reported missing."

"Who reported it?"

"Her maid. Said she expected her mistress in the early afternoon, and when night came with no word she called us. By then any passengers were of course long gone. We had to rouse the porter from his bed."

"If you suspect Watson and me of being the two mystery passengers I'm afraid I must disappoint you."

"No, of all the epithets I could apply to you, kidnapper of women is not one. Your name has arisen in the investigation, however."

"How so?"

"It seems that while Michael Donalson, Professor of Botany, was away in Peru on a research trip, Mrs, Donalson has had a suitor."

"I assure you that you are looking at a man innocent of that indiscretion. Watson!"

"Why, Holmes, we haven't even met the lady!"

"You see inspector, between the two of us we lack motive and opportunity."

"We know who the suitor was, Professor Ven Dreisling."

"I'm not sure if you have heard, but yesterday evening the Professor was a bit too all over the place to make love to a colleague's wife."

"Yes, but as our investigations overlap…"

"I do not have an investigation at the moment."

"What? You aren't investigating the Ven Dreisling murder?"

"What is left to investigate? Actually placing cuffs on the guilty party is your job."

"But in Professor Donalson we have a potentially jealous husband…"

"And a professional rival, both possible motives. Let me ask two questions."

"By all means."

"Is Professor Donalson twelve feet tall?"

"I, I suppose I don't know for certain, but that seems like the kind of thing that would have been mentioned. We searched their home and I didn't remember giant clothes."

"Second, is he in Peru?"

"Sorry?"

"He is meant to be on an expedition in Peru, correct? Is he there? If so, I'd say that clears him. Wire the British Embassy. Have them check their travel records."

"Fine, I'll do that. But, what now?"

"Now, I see Mrs. Hudson has my eggs ready. Call on me tomorrow, Inspector, I shall endeavour to have some news for you."

After his breakfast Holmes retired to his quarters and I settled into my writing. Later there was a rapping at the door and I heard Mrs. Hudson answer.

"Go away you filthy tramp!" she yelled.

"Now, Mrs. I'm just trying to make enough for a warm meal. A ha'penny for this fine pencil, the same type Her Majesty uses incidentally."

"I'll not be harassed by vagrants in my own home!"

"I'd never harass a beautiful creature such as yourself. How about a flower, missus? Picked it right from the City Park, just for you."

"Get your hands off of me you masher!"

At that my blood boiled. Taking liberties with poor Mrs. Hudson that I would not stand for. I stomped down the stairs,

121

took the wretch by the collar and brought my fist back. He laughed. The degenerate mendicant actually laughed! I swung with all my might, but the man pushed my arm away, wrapped his own arm around it and leveraged himself against me somehow.

"There, there, Watson. I believe Mrs. Hudson's honour has been defended."

"Holmes! Someday the joke will be on you!"

"Gave me a right fright you did, Mr. Holmes. Now where's my flowers?" Holmes laughed and produced a bouquet from beneath his filthy coat.

"Are these really from the magic forest in the Park?"

"I can't speak to magic but the Park is indeed overgrown. It is a sight to behold!"

"You needed this getup to go to the park?"

"No, I needed this getup to conduct my investigation at the train station."

"I'd rather think porters and bums are natural enemies."

"Quite so."

"I don't understand."

"The police, as uniformed men themselves, are trained to look for buttons and brass and shined shoes. They no doubt did an admirable job of interrogating the railway employees. They, like most, failed to even notice the actual denizens of the station. These downtrodden transients were more than happy to redress a thousand perceived wrongs done to them by the railway by spilling every secret thing they had seen in and about the station, to another of their kind."

"Did they see what happened to Mrs. Donalson?"

"Yes."

"Well? Out with it Mr. Holmes! You owe an old lady that much after the fright you gave me."

"While the railway staff were focused on unloading the passengers onto the platform, on the far side of the train an apparently unconscious woman was passed through a window to two men dressed in black. Two more men climbed out of the window after her. Each man grabbed a limb and they ran out the back of the station to a waiting carriage."

"No one saw this?"

"No one but the station dwellers, who populate every nook of the place. The abduction took place in the narrow space between two parallel trains. One empty and the other disembarking. Besides, you know how railway travellers are, focused only on the next destination, oblivious to all that surrounds them."

"That's all well and good Mr. Holmes, but where is the lady?"

"I do not know, Mrs. Hudson. She could be anywhere in London, indeed by this time anywhere in England."

"You've got an uncharacteristic spring in your step for being in the dark on a case."

"Not quite in the dark, Watson. In fact, thanks to some missionaries out to preach the good word even to a tramp like myself, I've seen the light!"

"Just when I thought a murderous giant was the most remarkable thing I would see all week!"

Holmes produced a religious pamphlet from the breast of his filthy jacket and smacked it across his other palm. I pulled it from his grasp. In garish typeface it declared new prosperity under the beneficent gaze of the Green Man. New vitality, prosperity and fecundity for those that would swear the green.

"Holmes, this is the worst kind of poppycock!"

"Yes, but it is the worst kind of poppycock taking place at midnight tonight in the City Park." He pointed at the back of the pamphlet. "Rarely do we have villains so considerate as to invite us to their crimes. We shall have to oblige, Watson."

"Who is this Green Man, anyway?" asked Mrs. Hudson, now pursuing the pamphlet.

"I don't think it is a name so much as a title. Rather like the Freemasons for those that work with plants rather than bricks."

"Really, Holmes?"

"There are hundreds of these pseudo-occult secrets societies in England. Rather a knee-jerk reaction to the modern age I should think."

"So you think Mrs. Donalson has been kidnapped by a secret society of florists?"

"More likely botanists, like her husband and Ven Dreisling."

"To what end?"

"If we hadn't born witness to Ven Dreisling grizzly demise I would chalk it up to some sort of fraternal jape, an initiation ceremony perhaps. But here as in many things I fear that a group of woolly-headed individuals has fallen for their own claptrap and now intends to perform some ritualistic murder."

"Murder!" Mrs. Hudson fell back in her chair.

"Many of these societies are built around pantomimes of supposedly ancient ceremonies. Symbolic murders and resurrections and the like. This pamphlet is just the right mix of occult nostalgia and religious nonsense for one of these organizations. Only they have forgotten they are play acting."

"I shall clean my service revolver and stand in readiness."

"Good man, I shall contact Inspector Gregson. I can put his lack of imagination and subtlety to good use tonight."

Mrs. Hudson cooked a hearty vegetable stew at Holmes's request. The joke seemed juvenile but as long as Holmes was in high spirits I felt we had nothing to fear. While the pot boiled on the stove Holmes' scrubbed away his disguise and I lovingly oiled my Webley in preparation for tonight. After dinner I played Mrs. Hudson at draughts while Holmes picked jauntily at his violin. Soon the hand of the clocked ticked round to half past eleven.

"I would have thought Inspector Gregson would have been here by now." I said as Mrs. Hudson captured my last piece.

"I'm afraid the Inspector is occupied at the moment." Holmes smiled to himself.

"We're taking on this Green Man cult alone, then?"

"I wouldn't dream of it, Watson. The London constabulary will be there in full force."

"That's all right, then, I suppose." I said, trying to decipher Holmes' Sphinx-like expression. We pulled on our coats, hats, and at Holmes' insistence, wellies, and made our way out into the night. Mrs. Hudson gave us one last admonition to be careful.

The streets were strangely deserted and I kept my hand on the grip of my gun as we made our way in silence. Our steps seemed to echo and the mist clinging to the ground only increased the eerie ambience. My first sight of the forest that had grown up in City Park forced a gasp that seemed like a shout against the silence. Holmes gave me a sideways glance and then pushed aside some vegetation and began picking his way through. The gaslights in the park, through overgrown, still worked, casting a hundred strange shadows everywhere. I focused on the Inverness cape of my friend and put one foot in front of another. Soon we heard voices. I pulled my gun but Holmes waved for me to put it back. To my surprise he stepped openly into the clearing ahead and announced 'vivat hortus regnum'.

"Welcome, brother." said a voice. More murmured in agreement.

"My friend," Holmes gestured towards me. "I have told him of the Green Man and he is eager to learn more." I stepped from the bush and was warmly greeted. Then there was a commotion from the other side of the clearing. Four men carrying something large and thrashing. My first thought was some sort of albino deer, but then I saw it to be a woman in a white robe, her hands and feet bound, her mouth gagged. There was no mistaking the meaning of the muffled screams, or the look of terror in her eyes. I went for my gun but again Holmes stayed me.

"Holmes, how can you…"

"Trust in me, Watson. Our true quarry has yet to appear." To the approval of the gathered crowd the men now cut her binds and forced her to lay splayed across the large stone sundial at the centre of the park. They bound her hand and foot to the pedestal of the sundial. Still she thrashed and screamed. The assembled formed a wide circle around the clearing and the four men began a call and response liturgy. As the strange ceremony progressed the foliage behind the sundial began to

125

shudder and shake. The group became louder and louder until suddenly rose up a giant figure covered in leaves and vines. The figure roared and the crowd cheered. Mrs. Donalson yanked frantically at her bindings.

"Now, Watson!"

I pulled my revolver and fired, striking the figure full in the chest. There was no reaction. I fired another shot to the chest. The figure moved toward the sundial, some alien lasciviousness emanating from his leafy form. I fired for the head, nothing slowed the figure.

"I may have been hasty in my assumption that Green Man was in fact a man." Holmes said. Mrs. Donalson had worked her gag free and was now openly screaming.

"We have to do something!" I seized Holmes by the shoulder. He looked back behind us and then scanned the rest of the clearing. I felt him slump a little beneath his cape.

"Right, if bullets aren't working..." he pulled his sword free of his walking stick. The metallic shing rang in the air. Some of the assembled people looked over in confusion. Holmes rushed forward and drove his blade into the belly of the beast. It reared back and roared in rage. Holmes pulled the sword back out and made a swipe across the belly this time as if to disembowel it. The fearsome giant bellowed and then seized Holmes by the chest. I could tell by the way Holmes was frantically tugging at the monster's giant hand that he was being crushed. His sword had fallen to the ground. I began to step towards it when all of a sudden the Green Man was screeching in horrible pain and dropped Holmes. His followers looked around in confusion. There was a strange chemical smell in the air.

"Cover your face, Watson!" Holmes wheezed from the ground. He was fiddling with the pocket of his jacket. I kneeled down next to him and freed his handkerchief. I pressed it to his face and then pressed his hands to the handkerchief. He nodded in thanks. I then pulled forth my own handkerchief and covered my own face. As I looked around many of the gathered crowd were doing the same. The few who did not were now bent over coughing. The Green Man had contorted over backwards writhing in pain. Its awful dry scream was filling my head until I could think of nothing else.

From out of the trees stepped a dozen constables wearing gas masks. On their back they wore metal tanks, and they each held out some sort of dispersement device, spraying all of the plant life as they moved in. Once in the clearing they began securing the assembled party. Remembering poor Mrs. Donalson I quickly leapt up and ran to her. She lay unmoving upon the sundial, but her bosom still rose and fell. I took her delicate face in my hand and felt for a pulse at her neck. Her eyelids opened heavily for just a moment and her lips parted in what appeared to me to be a thanks. I undid her bonds and laid her down on the ground beneath the chemical cloud. Holmes had staggered over to the body of the Green Man, now just a macabre topiary. He plunged his hand into the chest and came out holding some giant seed. He stuffed it under his cape just before Inspector Gregson appeared.

"Hallo, boys!" he clapped Holmes on the back. Holmes sputtered and gasped and fell to the ground again. "Looks like that good old Inspector Gregson just saved your lives, eh!"

"I'm not sure spraying someone with a chemical killing agent quite qualifies as lifesaving." Holmes rasped.

"Now, now, no need to be sore. Your little tip proved helpful. Although it is not like we would have missed this lot."

"I have no doubt that you would have eventually discovered the rampaging, magic fuelled mob that was moments away from issuing from this park. However, thanks to me you found them before an innocent woman was murdered, before the Green Man could gorge himself on the blood of an innocent, and before the cult members was bound together in dark magic."

"Let's not get ahead of ourselves with presumptions, Mr. Holmes. What matters here is that I successfully lead the London Police in a raid upon a dangerous organization and thereby rescued a missing woman. The rest is conjecture and fancy. Don't worry, Mr. Holmes, I shall credit you for your little tip in the final report." With that Inspector Gregson wandered off barking arbitrary orders at random constables.

"What little tip was that?" I asked Holmes.

"I notified the good Inspector of this gathering, and suggested he could best put a stop to it by spraying down the plant life here in the park with the defoliant kept at the Royal Botanical Society. I suggested further that the Society hall would be all but vacant because all of the members would be here."

"All but vacant?"

"It was my belief, borne out tonight, that the founding membership of the Green Man cult was much the same as the membership of the Royal Botanical Society."

"Much the same? Then why were we allowed to attend the ritual murder of Professor Van Dreisling?"

"Ah, because in situations like this there is always that one person who doesn't make the cut. In this case, that one person was the only one who didn't know better than to allow us to attend, and further to inspect the crime scene."

"You mean Professor Surell?"

"Yes, the poor Professor does not even know that he is the sap in some cruel social game at the Society. I wouldn't be surprised if he himself was not invited that night. Unless perhaps he was meant to be the sacrifice that evening."

"So you tasked Inspector Gregson with retrieving the defoliant?"

"Right before this ceremony, when I knew all guilty parties would be here. I guessed that Surell would be studying at the Society alone, for where else does a man like that have to go? The Inspector barrelled right into the Society hall, demanded the chemicals, and then tromped right over here, killing every plant in his path, no questions asked, good old Gregson."

"And the Green Man was tied to these plants?"

"I suspect these plants were actually part of Green Man. We think of individuals as distinct from each other, but that is a quirk of the animal kingdom. Plants often operate more as a collective. Killing those plants was like taking Green Man down by breaking one bone at a time."

"You disparaged Gregson for blindly massacring the plant life in the Park, but it seems like you knowingly and horribly destroyed a sentient being with as little remorse."

"Ah, not killed. The monster rests right here." He patted the giant seed he concealed. "The Green Man lived before the rise of mankind and I suspect will survive our fall. What injury can mortal men like ourselves do to a demigod?"

"Perhaps the more pressing question now is what injury can a demigod do to mortal men like us?"

Holmes just chuckled.

Robert Perret's Top Ten:

1. The Sign of Four
2. The Adventure of the Six Napoleons
3. The Hound of the Baskervilles
4. The Adventure of the Musgrave Ritual
5. The Adventures of the Engineer's Thumb
6. The Adventures of the Copper Beeches
7. The Man with the Twisted Lip
8. The Adventure of the Blue Carbuncle
9. The Adventure of the Solitary Cyclist
10. The Adventure of the Abbey Grange

Why Sherlock Holmes?...Margaret Walsh

I was asked a question recently that got me thinking. I was talking with someone who knows me, but only relatively recently. He was unaware of my dedication to Sherlock Holmes and was surprised when I told him about my story being included in this august volume. He asked me "Why Sherlock Holmes? Why that character, and not, say, Hercule Poirot?" I made a flippant remark and left it at that, but he really did get me thinking on the subject of my exposure to the Great Detective.

I can still remember the first Sherlock Holmes story I read. I was at my local library, desperately looking for something to read. I'd exhausted all the children's books, and my poor mother had had to join the library so I could get adult books to read. I was ten years old. This day, I was wandering disconsolately among the shelves unable to make a choice. The librarian, a neighbour of ours, took pity on me. She marched to the shelves, selected a book and handed it to me with the prophetic words "I know you'll enjoy this."

Doubtfully, I looked at the cover. It was '*A Study in Scarlet*'. I checked it out at took it home. Settling down to read it, I wasn't too enthralled, until I came to the passage where Stamford is explaining to Watson about Holmes beating a dead body with a stick to ascertain whether bruises can form after death. That was it. I was hooked. And when it got to the line "You have been in Afghanistan, I perceive", I was not only hooked, but reeled in and gaffed as well. The story was exciting, and intelligent, and the heroes were interesting. I say heroes, because it was immediately obvious to me that Holmes and Watson were a pair. You couldn't have one without the other.

Poirot can survive without his Hastings, but Holmes without Watson is like meat without salt.

I was back up at the library the next day to see if there were any more of these treasures. I happily carried home the library's entire collection of Sherlock Holmes stories. Seeing my enthusiasm, my father's Christmas gift to me that year was an omnibus edition of all the stories.

Why Sherlock Holmes? On the face of it a Victorian detective should hold no charms for a 20th century child growing into a 21st century woman. It's a question I have asked myself over and over again for the last 40 years. I've also realized that it isn't just a question for me. It is almost a universal question.

Holmes and Watson made an early transition to movies and to radio. For many people of a certain age, the first names they associate with the pairing is Basil Rathbone and Nigel Bruce. Then television, and Granada's wonderful adaptations of the canon with Jeremy Brett and David Burke/Edward Hardwicke, became the Holmes and Watson(s) for another generation. And the beat goes on. Each new Sherlock Holmes movie announcement is guaranteed an excited audience, whether for Robert Downey Junior, or Will Ferrell. There are TWO television partnerships with Benedict Cumberbatch and Martin Freeman in London, and Johnny Lee Miller and Lucy Liu in New York.

Then there is publishing. More pastiches have been published now than the original canon. Sherlock Holmes is there in traditional Arthur Conan Doyle style stories, in steampunk novels, or battling Lovecraft's eldritch gods. Every year I read at least ten new Sherlock Holmes books.

Finally, there is merchandise. Not just tie in stuff to the BBC's version, but much to be gathered and treasured by the dedicated Sherlockian. I have a tee shirt with a Sherlock Holmes quote on it purchased from the British Library, postcards of some of Sidney Paget's illustrations purchased from the Museum of London, and not to mention my highly prized Sherlock Holmes rubber duck. I cannot think of any other literary creations that have spawned as much memorabilia as Holmes and Watson.

So the question remains: Why Sherlock Holmes?

132

It isn't the mysteries. Other writers have created stories as beguiling and as interesting as any Arthur Conan Doyle did. Agatha Christie's *'Murder on the Orient Express'* is a good case. At no point did Sherlock Holmes have to deal with a case where, quite literally, everybody did it. Margery Allingham's Albert Campion, and Dorothy L. Sayers' Lord Peter Wimsey all solved interesting and intricate mysteries. But none of them, not even Agatha Christie, has generated the level of obsession with the characters.

It certainly isn't the continuity, or lack thereof. Arthur Conan Doyle is pretty much a by word for how not to create a fictional world. Mrs Hudson mysteriously morphs into Mrs Turner in one story! He cannot seem to remember if Watson's first name is John or James! And please do NOT get me started on Watson's wonderful wandering war wound!

It isn't the depth of the supporting characters either, because most of them are pretty one dimensional. Holmes and Watson fairly blaze off the pages, leaving all the other characters in shadow. Even firm fan favourite Mrs Hudson doesn't get much of a look in in the original stories. It took movies and television to flesh her out. Irene Handl in 'The Private Life of Sherlock Holmes' and Una Stubbs in BBC's 'Sherlock' are arguably the two portrayals that have given this character the most life.

So what is left? What is it that makes Sherlock Holmes so readable, relatable, and thoroughly enjoyable as much in the 21st century as it was in the 19th?

The answer, to me, is friendship.

It seems to me that Sherlock Holmes and John Watson are archetypes for friendship. The friendship the characters had formed by the end of 'A Study in Scarlet' drew me in. I mentioned Poirot and Hastings before. Hastings is the sidekick. He is there to provide an audience for Poirot's brilliance. Hastings is not an equal partner in the enterprise. It is the same in many other detective pairings. But not with Holmes and Watson. You cannot have one without the other. Holmes says it himself: "I would be lost without my Boswell."

It is possibly the most intense friendship in literature. It is the friendship we all secretly desire. Someone who would give their life for us, and that we would do the same for. It is a friendship shown most clearly in that most moving of passages from '*The Adventure of the Three Garridebs*': "My friend's wiry arms were around me and he was leading me to the chair. "You're not hurt, Watson? For God's sake say that you're not hurt!" It was worth a wound - it was worth many wounds - to know the depth of loyalty and love which lay beyond that cold mask. The clear, hard eyes were dimmed for a moment, and the firm lips were shaking. For the one and only time I caught a glimpse of a great heart as well as of a great brain."

It's a friendship that has the ring of truth about it, based as it is on honesty. Holmes and Watson both have their vices and virtues. One of their earliest exchanges in 'A Study in Scarlet' has both men laying forth their worst habits: "Let me see—what are my other shortcomings? I get in the dumps at times, and don't open my mouth for days on end. You must not think I am sulky when I do that. Just let me alone, and I'll soon be right. What have you to confess now? It's just as well for two fellows to know the worst of one another before they begin to live together."

I laughed at this cross-examination. "I keep a bull pup," I said, "and I object to rows because my nerves are shaken, and I get up at all sorts of ungodly hours, and I am extremely lazy. I have another set of vices when I'm well, but those are the principal ones at present."

Of course Holmes failed to mention several other habits, as Watson notes in '*The Musgrave Ritual*' for example: "I have always held, too, that pistol practice should be distinctly an open-air pastime; and when Holmes, in one of his queer humours, would sit in an armchair with his hair-trigger and a hundred Boxer cartridges and proceed to adorn the opposite wall with a patriotic V.R. done in bullet pocks, I felt strongly that neither the atmosphere nor the appearance of our room was improved by it." Strong onscreen chemistry between various Holmes and Watsons has helped keep the character's flame alive. Jeremy Brett and David Burke, followed by Jeremy Brett and Edward Hardwicke had perfect onscreen vibes. In later years Robert Downey Junior and Jude Law sparkled on the big screen. And the chemistry between Benedict Cumberbatch and Martin Freeman can only be described as superb.

Sherlock Holmes and John Watson are two people who understand each other perfectly. It's not a perfect friendship, no friendship is, but it is, I think, an ideal that people aspire to. A friendship based on loyalty, trust, humour, and love. We all want it, and because it is so rare, we find stories about such a pair of friends to be irresistible. The relationship that is friendship hasn't changed in hundreds of years, leaving the Sherlock Holmes stories as strong and as fresh as when they first appeared in Strand Magazine.

'What is it, Holmes?'
'It's a floor, Watson.'

The Chess Game....Danielle Gastineau

(*From the Memoirs of Dr. John H. Watson M.D.*)

It was late in the evening on April 20th 1886 and I was making my way home to Baker Street tired and worn out from a long, long day. I had three surgeries that day and whilst two were successful the third, sadly, was not. With a slow, measured tread I entered the home I shared with my friend, Mr. Sherlock Holmes and found him along with our landlady Mrs. Hudson and her thirteen-year-old granddaughter Molly sitting in the ground floor sitting-room which was part of Mrs Hudson's domain.

The room was medium sized with whitewashed walls, a fireplace with photos and small figurines on the mantelpiece. The couch that Mrs. Hudson was sitting on was green and blue and on both sides of this were two matching chairs, Mrs. Hudson was sewing what appeared to be one of Holmes's shirts. Molly and Holmes were seated at a medium sized table that had a white table cloth on it, the two were playing chess and from what I could see Molly was clearly winning. Whether he letting her win, which I strongly suspected, was yet to be determined.

Mrs. Hudson poured me some most welcome tea and I told her about my day and she offered me some wise and helpful words that made me smile. Holmes and Molly were talking about the things she had been learning in school, she told him about a boy she liked and he told her she wasn't allowed to marry until she was at least fifty, this made her laugh. Molly had brown hair and brown eyes and was wearing a grey and blue dress, her parents owned the Baker Street Bakery and were out visiting some friends.

"Checkmate," Molly said with a smile.

"Perhaps I let you win," Holmes teased her.

"No, I won fair and square," Molly told him with a smile.

"Yes, you did, you did very well," Holmes smiled. "How did you do it?"

"A chess player never reveals her secrets," Molly replied with a smile. "Another game?"

"No, I think it's time for this little chess player to go to bed," Mrs. Hudson told her granddaughter.

"Can't I stay up longer?" Molly asked her.

"It's nearly nine o' clock and way past your bedtime, young lady." Mrs. Hudson told her.

Molly wished them good night and went to her room which was the guestroom on the first floor next to Mrs. Hudson bedroom. About a half hour later I was heading up to my room when I saw Holmes heading into his room and I followed him.

"Holmes," I stood at the door frame. "You really didn't just let her win, did you?"

"No, she won fair and square as she said." Holmes smiled and got out his pipe, he never smoked in proximity to Molly. "I should thank her father for teaching her those tricks."

"How did you know he's been teaching her?" I asked.

"The other day when I had occasion to look for Mrs. Hudson. Molly and her friend Dawn were ensconced in the kitchen talking and I overheard Molly tell Dawn that her father had been teaching her secret chess moves he learned from his grandfather. I really should have known better than to engage her in a battle. To be beaten by a child," he sighed, shaking his head ruefully.

I couldn't help but laugh a little.

"Goodnight Holmes" I smiled.

"Goodnight Watson" Holmes replied.

A Cricketing Interlude....David Ruffle

An excerpt from the yet to be published, 'Sherlock Holmes and the Scarborough Affair' in which Watson meets one of his heroes.

The events in the hotel had certainly lessened my enthusiasm for cricket watching although not diminished it altogether. In any case, it was taken out of my hands on the first day of the festival for heavy rain was brought in by gale force winds and there was no hope of any cricket being played. Holmes had been desirous of my services the following day, limited though they may have been. On the third morning however, Holmes was nowhere to be found and as he had left no instructions for me I decided that a day at the Scarborough Festival was just what I needed.

I was to be amply rewarded for I had the opportunity to see Wilfred Rhodes score a sparkling century for Yorkshire against the MCC. It was a faultless innings of 105, only ending when he misjudged a ball from Holloway and was bowled through his legs. His look of disappointment as he made way back to the pavilion mirrored my own to perfection. Another hour or so watching the man bat would have been delightful.

By chance the following morning after a welcome coffee in the lounge I happened to look through the doorway of the Cricketers' Room and there spied Wilfred Rhodes deep in thought in one of the armchairs. I was somewhat hesitant about approaching him for I had heard tales that the man could be most dour and taciturn, but the opportunity of talking to one of my sporting heroes far outweighed any notion of etiquette.

139

"Excuse me, Mr Rhodes, I wonder if I could join you for a few moments. I witnessed your century yesterday and would like to express my admiration at your play. It was a pleasure to watch."

"Aye, lad, sit yoursen down, it's a free country after all. Aye, it were a good days' play were yesterday, thank you for your appreciation. What fettle?"

"Fettle? Oh, I think I have it. I am very well thank you, and you?"

"Can't complain, lad."

"My name is Watson, Doctor Watson," I said, as I made myself comfortable in an armchair opposite the great man.

"'Ow do."

"I noticed that although you scored quickly yesterday there were some strokes that I was surprised you did not employ."

"Oh, aye?"

"The cut for one."

"Ah well, Doctor, the cut was nivver a business stroke were it? Not for me any road. Some players' allus want to use it, but not me, nivver."

"But surely it's a useful stroke for scoring quickly and keeping the fielders on their toes."

"'Appen you may be right, but it's finished many an innings for some batters. Cricket's not for laiking about tha knows, it's work; I have my shillings to earn."

"The Festival is different surely? The whole premise of it is built on the enjoyment of watching free-flowing and entertaining cricket."

"That's as mebbe, but anyroad I reckon you had your money's worth out of me, Doc," he replied with a smile.

"That is very true. Have you any heroes yourself within cricket, Mr Rhodes?"

"I'll tell thee what lad, I am lucky to be in the same side as some grand lads. Take Georgie Hirst, a good bat and a good bowler, different as chalk n' cheese us, but he's a good lad."

"I was fortunate enough to see Victor Trumper score his triple century against Sussex two years ago, it was a memorable innings. You've played against him of course."

"Aye, well that Victor, he's a good bat."

"In the same match we witnessed some great play by CB Fry."

"Fry, he's a good bat. Ranji too, both good bats."

In Rhodes's vocabulary 'good' was evidently the absolute pinnacle of praise. There were no airs and graces attached to this forthright, but charming man. I asked him about the famed accuracy of his spin bowling.

"I read somewhere that you can drop the ball on a sixpence over after over, is that true?"

"Mebbe," he replied with a laugh, "I can keep it there or thereabouts."

"It must be terrifically hard on the fingers to be spinning the ball for any length of time."

"'Appen it is, but then I don't allus spin it."

"No?"

"No and I'll tell you why lad, if the batsman *thinks* ah'm spinning it then ah'm spinning it. They haven't always got the nouse to realise what ah'm up to."

"That's very canny of you Mr Rhodes."

"Aye, well I have my moments, lad. Ah'm not back'ard at comin' for'ard sometimes tha knows see thee?"

"I do see."

"I reckon I'll order missen a brew, lad."

I sensed the interview had come to an end. "Thank you for your time, Mr Rhodes, I have really enjoyed this talk with you."

"Likewise, Doc. Take care of thissen, put wood in'th oyle on way out, lad."

I interpreted these mystifying words as 'please close the door on your way out' and this I did.

The hotel was strangely quiet given the events of the last few days. The hustle and bustle so noticeable on our arrival had given way to a sombreness which reached and touched everyone. Poor Monsieur Poisvert gave me a half-hearted wave from the

141

reception area. I idly wondered whether his professional standing would ever recover from what had befallen his previously impeccably run hotel.

The Guilty Man...set by Mark Mower

Inspector Lestrade is investigating the murder of a wealthy businessman in a gentleman's club in Westminster. On the basis of the evidence available to him, he is convinced that one of four characters, arrested in the club at the time, is guilty of the crime.

During Lestrade's subsequent interrogations, the four men make the following statements:

Colonel Moran: *"Pietro Venucci killed him."*

Pietro Venucci: *"Colonel Moran killed him."*

John Clay: *"Pietro Venucci is telling the truth."*

Henry Peters: *"John Clay's not lying."*

With the other evidence he has assembled, Inspector Lestrade has reason to believe that three of these statements are untrue. If that is the case, which man is guilty of murder?

Criminal Links...Mark Mower

Solve the Crime Godoku puzzle below by completing the grid so that every row, column and three-by-three box contains one of nine individual letters. Some letters have already been provided and completion of the puzzle should reveal the name of a location that appears in *A Study in Scarlet*:

			S		A			
		T				O		
	S			R			A	
L	A						O	N
N				U				S
T	O						I	U
	L			S			T	
		A				L		
			O		R			

The Dare...Danielle Gastineau

Early one afternoon thirteen-year-old Molly Jones was standing, seemingly aimlessly, with the Baker Street Irregulars near the entrance to the Diogenes Club. She was wearing, rather bizarrely, a page boy uniform along with a cap covering her hair that had been put up in a bun by her friend, Kate. Kate was also responsible for her uniform that she had helped Molly on with in a nearby unoccupied building. Wiggins, the appointed leader of the Irregulars, had told her that if she wanted to continue to hang out with them then she had to prove her worth by delivering a message to Mr. Holmes's brother, Mycroft.

"What if I get caught?" Molly asked, "I could get into trouble. Girls are not allowed in the club, even I know that."

"If you do I'll take the fall for you," Wiggins told her with a smile. "Do this and you'll be one of us."

"I'll do it," Molly said firmly, taking the message from Wiggins.

She took a deep breath and walked into the imposing building. She entered the main lobby and found a short, stocky man sitting at a desk writing in a large book. She remembered what Billy had said about how to get to Mycroft's room and both disguising and lowering her voice, told the man, rather grandly, that she had a message for Mr Mycroft Holmes. The uniformed man, who was not paying much attention merely pointed her in the direction of the staircase.

She walked gingerly up the red carpeted staircase feeling very nervous, but it was too late to turn back now. She came to a large wooden door and taking another deep breath, entered a large room that was filled wall to wall with books, a fireplace, several tables with chairs drawn under them, a couch, and two chairs on either side of a fireplace. At a large window stood a man with white hair that she assumed was Mycroft.

"Mr. Holmes," Molly said nervously, forgetting all about the need to disguise her voice.

"Yes?" Mycroft said, turning and smiling. He was tall like his brother, but somewhat larger. "Thank you, young lady."

Molly froze where she stood, rooted to the spot.

"Don't tell please, Wiggins and Billy put me up to this." Molly felt like she was going to cry.

"Don't worry I won't say a word."Mycroft laughed and read the note

"How did you know I was a girl?" Molly asked

"Your voice and your cheekbones primarily, but there were several other signs," Mycroft replied. "What's your name?"

"Molly Jones," she replied."My grandmother is your brother's landlady."

"Oh," Mycroft said, writing a response to his brother's note. "So you are the clever young lady who beat my brother at chess."

"He told you?" Molly said a little surprised by the fact the younger Holmes talked about her.

"He also told me you also like breaking codes and cracking ciphers"

"Yes, my friend Dawn and me sometimes send each other messages that way," Molly told him, her eyes widening as he pressed a note and three shiny tanners into her hand

"The sixpences are for you, my dear. Anyone who can fool old Franklin downstairs deserves a little extra," Mycroft said, with a little laugh.

"Thank you," Molly squealed. "I should probably get going before Wiggins sends the Irregulars in to look for me!"

"Your secret is safe with me," Mycroft told her with a smile.

"Thank you," Molly said, turning to go.

Wiggins and Billy were waiting outside and Kate was starting to get worried when they saw Molly running towards them. Molly didn't tell them what had happened; she just handed Billy the message and he made his way back to Baker Street. Kate took Molly back to the empty building to get her back into her normal clothes.

When she returned to her parent's bakery her mother gave her a small package of freshly baked rolls with instructions to take them to her grandmother. She walked up to the door of 221b Baker Street just as Sherlock Holmes and Dr Watson were leaving.

"What have you been up to all day then Molly?" Dr Watson asked.

"I have been at my friend Dawn's house," Molly replied.

"I thought she was in America," Dr Watson said.

"Oh...er...she came back last night." She said, noticing the questioning look on Holmes's face."I have to go and give these rolls to my grandmother".

The two men watched as Molly quickly made her way inside the house.

"She may be a budding code breaker, but she is a very bad liar," said Holmes, laughing to himself as he hailed a cab.

Singapore Sling....Anna Lord

Many had entered the Pit of Death. None had ever left under their own steam.

How had it come to this?

Dr Watson's heart banged against the walls of his ribcage like a clenched fist banging against the walls of a prison. Prickly hot sweat was pouring down his back in feverish rivulets. He gulped a mouthful of steamy air that burned his throat and lungs.

This was *not* how he pictured his ending. He imagined something noble...heroic...

Determined not to disgrace himself, he tried to stand up – to give himself a fighting chance - but his head reeled as he swayed like a palm in a tropical monsoon. Memories were coming thick and fast now that the blood had returned to his brain; memories clouded with opium dens and red lanterns. The visions were a vice-ridden haze of incense dreams full of hungry ghosts that floated across his retina like Chinese laundry flapping above the crowded streets where hawkers sold curry by the roadside, and bullock drays vied with rickshaw wallahs, and the smell of joss sticks mingled with hell money burning in front of makeshift shrines to ward off demons. His mouth felt ashen. His tongue cleaved to the roof of his mouth.

There was the putrid taste of tainted laksa on his tongue, metallic, sickly, rancid, it made him want to vomit – and then he did. Fear did that too. He legs felt weak, his hands were trembling. Steadying, he wiped some spicy spittle from his lips.

A gin sling – that's what he needed to wash the acrid taste of fear from his mouth - a dash of lime, a squeeze of fresh lemon... add some ice cubes to make pearls glisten on the frosty high-ball glass. Chin-chin!

In the Far East death was white. And so were the ghosts of all the girls who smelled of cannabis flowers and tasted like jackfruit. Cantonese and Hokkien goddesses were reserved for the Chinese pangs, the triads, the guilds, and the secret societies that controlled everything east of Eden. Karayuki-san were for the rest. They all had coral smiles.

The dance floor was dirty. It was stained with something reddish that looked like dried-out laterite mud and smelled like the cloying resin from the rosewood tree. The walls of his cage were made of thick bamboo secured with rattan. Impossibly high. Impregnable. A roof of corrugated tin trapped him inside. There was no escape. He tried not to shiver like the poor terrified dogs on the menu in the marketplace near Sailor Town. He tried not to wet himself.

How did it come to this?

Yesterday it was high-tea in the Tiffin Tearoom of Raffles Hotel with the Sarkies Brothers, and a black-tie dinner to celebrate the capture of the Giant Rat of Singapore and then it was...

He couldn't remember anything after that. Someone slipped a narcotic into his G&T. He blacked out. And woke up in hell...

Where was Sherlock? Was that the blood of an Englishman on the perfumed floor of the Pit of Death? Had the great detective already battled with the Devil...and lost? Would they be fishing his mutilated remains out of the Rochor Canal tomorrow morning?

Someone was opening the door to the small dark tunnel from whence would emerge the fearsome creature with gnashing teeth and razor-sharp claws.

The rabid roar of the bear-baiting crowd forced his focus. A wall of demonic black eyes met him. He recognised Chinese, Sinhalese, Siamese, Tamils, Malays, and more. There were Australian seamen, American traders, British civil servants, and even some men from Her Majesty's Navy still in uniform. All there! All baying for blood! Money changed hands faster than a volley from a Martini-Henry rifle. The odds were stacked against him.

A dozen rats spewed forth from the maw and swarmed the pit, sniffing the evil air, the dried puke, the stale blood, the rust-red mud, the palpable fear in his veins. They were a warm-up to the main event. He realised now why the rosewood platform inside the pit was called a dance floor. He hopped from foot to foot to avoid being bitten. The threat of bubonic plague and rabies crossed his mind. It galvanised him into a frenzied dance macabre.

One desperate rat found its way inside his trouser leg. It clawed its way up. Someone tossed a small Chinese dagger through an opening in the cage. It clanked to the ground, sending rats scurrying for cover. He made a frantic grab, straightened up, and stabbed wildly at his own leg to stop the mad creature going all the way up to his groin. Stab! Stab! Stab! His leg was a bloody mess, throbbing with pain, but the creature lost its grip and slipped out. A red slick trickled down his leg and filled his shoe.

Another rat tried to take its place. He jumped and shook it off and stomped down hard. The crunch of bone and the squelch of fatty gore were drowned out by the screams of feral spectators who roared with delight. A cacophony of dialects clashed with hoots and cheers.

Watson!

Someone called out his name. Someone was rooting for him. It gave him courage. It gave him strength. He scanned the sea of slanty eyeballs, *mata-mata* burning like black coals in the pit of hell, and recognised Miss Luxi Gong, the attractive teapot curator who had been trafficked to white slavers. Was she the next act? She was white as a ghost already, standing in the shadow of Madame Fang who was clutching a yapping Pekinese to her sexless breast.

Watson!

Again, he heard the name above the din. For a moment he seemed to recognise it; a voice from the past. He thought it might be Dr Hu, but no, the inscrutable Feng Shui master was standing on a wooden tea chest at the back of the crowd, too far back to make himself heard.

Ouch! He kicked and stabbed and stomped until the rats were beaten, lying dead and bleeding around the edges of the cage. By the time he'd finished he was breathing so hard he wondered if his heart might burst.

Watson!

Was he delirious? Was he hearing things? He spotted Colonel Bulwer Cumberbutch at the front of the crowd. The cocksure villain was grinning from ear to ear. His court case had been postponed. There was talk he would walk free. Major Hartlepoole of the Detective Branch of the Straits Settlement Police Force had been bribed. It was rumoured his venal hand was behind the 1891 explosion in the forecourt of Police Headquarters. There he was, standing behind the colonel, corrupt to the eyeballs.

Watson! Opium! It's on your clothes! Hurry! You must remove…

There was a moment of cognitive dissonance. Only one person called him Watson. He recognised the voice clearly this time. But the words were emanating from the twisted lips of a back-bent coolie, grimed with the filth of the streets. It didn't make sense.

Opium?

No, no, it was nutmeg. He'd gotten the aromatic powdery stuff on his clothes the day before yesterday when they visited the nutmeg plantation that belonged to Dr Verhoeven, the Dutch Naturalist who had delivered the lecture on orang-utans to the National Geographic Society. The specks had turned white in the heat. Everything in Singapore turned white: hungry ghosts, lotus blooms, opium powder, and Death.

A terrifying satanic screech froze the blood in his veins despite the fierce heat. And then Beelzebub's pup appeared in the flesh… The Giant Rat of Singapore, which was in fact a carnivorous marsupial from the hinterland of Tasmania, a stocky creature with a huge head and a thick neck. Forelegs longer than hind legs thrust the muscular body forward to produce a shuffling gait: the ferocious Tasmanian devil.

Sarcophilus satanicus (satanic meat-lover), a natural scavenger with powerful jaws and large teeth, it tore at the rats, devouring bone and fur... then turned to him, sniffing, sniffing. What could it smell? Nutmeg?

Diabolus ursinus (bear devil), it was giving off a pungent odour and frothing at the mouth. He'd seen that recently somewhere. That's right. Now he remembered. Dr Verhoeven had been conducting an experiment. A hunting dog had been fed raw opium for weeks...

Oh, my God! That's what Sherlock meant. The Devil was addicted to opium. And once addicted, it became deranged if the drug was withheld. And now! The white stuff was on his clothes. Someone had sprinkled it on him while he lay unconscious.

Opium!

As the Devil ran in circles, gorging on dead rats, desperate for the drug to assuage its agonised addiction, Dr Watson whipped off his jacket and tossed it on top of the demented creature. There was the sound of shredding and tearing as it fought with the garment before surfacing madder than ever, eyes fulgid, jaws foaming.

Arrows of pain shot up the doctor's legs as he kicked off his shoes and dropped his trousers and tossed them across the cage. With a disturbing screech, the ravenous creature chased after them and gorged on the fabric with a ferocity that was sickening to witness, grunting, gagging, choking; greedily mopping up every speck of white powder.

Tropical heat, coupled with the narcotic he'd been given, made the doctor sluggish but the shirt came next. He dropped the dagger as he snapped the buttons and jerked himself out of the sleeves while baby Beelzebub devoured a blood-soaked shoe.

He was standing in nothing more than his singlet and long-johns, his injured leg a coagulate mess, when the Devil turned and let out a high-pitched screech that reverberated to the very depths of hell.

Dr Watson, a reasonably fit man for his age despite all he had been through, with the physique of an ex-soldier, and never a coward, lunged for the dagger as the Devil charged. The blade struck home. The pitiful creature gave out a blood-curdling cry and fell to the ground where it shuddered and spasmed, writhing in appalling agony for one long terrible moment.

A police whistle shrilled. Uniformed officers rushed in. They were joined by her Majesty's finest.

Dr Hu plucked an axe out of thin air. It sailed over the heads of the panicked spectators and struck the bamboo cage. The back-bent coolie with the grimy face belted Colonel Cumberbutch on the chin and a brawl erupted. Everyone went berserk. Madame Fang's gang spirited her away through a back door. Miss Luxi Gong fainted. The filthy coolie grabbed the axe and broke through the bamboo cage.

"Watson!" he said, clasping his hand and holding on tight as if he was unlikely to ever let go. "Watson!"

Dr Watson felt choked. He could hardly breathe. He gazed upon the grimy face of his dearest friend and he could have sworn the lanceolate grey eyes were welling with emotion but, before he could confirm as much, the great detective snatched up the axe and sent it hurtling through the air. It struck Major Hartlepoole on the back – only with the blunt end – and brought him down like a nine pin before he could reach the exit. There'd be no evading justice this time, and there'd be no one for Colonel Bulwer Cumberbutch to bribe either. They were both going to spend a long time at her Majesty's pleasure.

As for Dr Verhoeven. His days as a white slaver were over. He had been arrested and charged. There would be a nice cell in Outram Prison for him too.

And the life-saving dagger?

"Not me," said Sherlock. "When I arrived at the scene you already had it in hand."

Dr Watson scratched his head, perplexed. "It must have been Madame Fang," he reasoned. "But why? Why would she want to give *me* a fighting chance?"

"I deduce she might be after a concession to farm opium, alcohol, and tobacco. It's all perfectly legal as long as she has a British licence. Now that Dr Verhoeven, Colonel Cumberbutch and Major Hartlepoole are out of the way, there'll be no stopping her. One day she will be the Guan Yu of the Colonial East and we will kow-tow to her. Now, my brave friend, let's get you some medical attention. And then we can enjoy a refreshing drink in the Raffles Bar. They have a new cocktail. It's disgustingly sweet. If they had any sense they'd name a cocktail after you, seriously, something with vim and vigour – a Watson Long-John!"

Dr Watson laughed until it hurt. "Who knows? One day they may even name a cocktail in your honour – something dry and bitter: a Sherlock Sour!"

'What is it, Holmes?'

'It's a pipe, Watson.'

The Paint Job...Danielle Gastineau

Mrs. Hudson had finally come to some kind of breaking point as she stared long and hard at the wall in Holmes's sitting-room and saw the initials V.R. marked out in bullet holes. Normally she would just ignore it, arrange to have the wall painted and add the paint materials to Holmes's rent, but this was the third time this year. She smiled when the idea came to her. She went to find Billy the page boy and asked him to go down and get some paint supplies, he asked her if she needed help painting the wall.

"No," Mrs. Hudson smiled. "I'm going to have Mr. Holmes clear up this mess himself."

About twenty or so minutes later Billy returned with the supplies; new brushes and yet another can of paint. He helped her lay out some newspapers on the table and they put the paint and materials on top of the newspapers. When Holmes and Dr Watson returned from the Turkish Baths they found Mrs. Hudson sitting in the basket-chair, sipping brandy from a glass. Then they saw the paint and brushes. Holmes looked quizzically at her.

"Are you intending to paint the room?" Holmes asked.

"Actually, no," Mrs. Hudson replied, "You, in fact, Mr. Holmes are going to paint over the VR you have once again decided to emblazon on the wall."

"I have a case in hand, can't it wait?" Holmes smiled at his landlady.

"No, it cannot wait. I am the end of my tether," Mrs. Hudson told him. "It shouldn't take you very long especially if the doctor assists you and once you have finished I will prepare your favourite meal."

"Roast beef and potatoes with Yorkshire pudding?" Holmes asked, smiling.

156

"Yes and green peas," Mrs. Hudson replied

"Watson, would you care to help me move the furniture?'

With the furniture moved away from the wall Holmes and a reluctant Watson rolled up their sleeves and got to work. Within an hour the wall was good as new and as promised Mrs. Hudson made them roast beef for dinner and the next time Holmes has the notion to shoot holes in the wall, you can be sure that there will be a paint can and a brush waiting on the table.

The Invisible Murderer......Soham Bagchi

NOTE: The Imperial Faberge eggs are a lost Scottish treasure of the eighteenth century.

SCENE 1: A small flat room, a fireplace, a table, a mirror, few odd looking ornaments and two sofas placed face to face on an old carpet. John sits on one sofa and Sherlock sits on the other with his legs up, having tea.

John: Why aren't you drinking?

Sherlock: I'm BORED! (*Then he takes his laptop from the table and opens it to check his mails*)

John: What is it? (*noticing his expression*)

Sherlock: Oh! I have got something interesting. (*sarcastically, then he reads an mail*)

Dear Mr. Holmes,

I am writing to you with a great emergency. Only you can save me. I am not able to sleep for last few days. I feel I am visited by ghosts. My wife died forty years ago. We went to see a rally and she disappeared from there. Her body was never recovered. I want you to investigate as you have a very 'keen investigative mind'. I have sent you a photo of her from that day. From Mr. Dean Whitaker.

(then he turns the screen and shows a photo of a blonde woman standing in a crowd)

John: Well, you must take the case. *(he laughs, Sherlock gives him a dirty look)*I forgot to tell you that Lestrade called when you were in the shower. He has asked you to go to the National Museum and join him there.

Sherlock: *(stands up enthusiastically and closes button of his coat)* Let's go then. Hope they have something interesting this time. *(Sherlock leaves the room and John follows him)*

SCENE 2:Inside the staff washroom of National Museum. John and Sherlock are accompanied by Lestrade.

Sherlock: How did it happen?

Lestrade: What?

Sherlock: You called me to the museum then you bring directly me to the staff washroom secured by the means of crime scene tape, so obviously some staff member has been murdered. Now tell me, how did it happen?

Lestrade: It's the security guard. He came here to take a bath after his shift. He was stabbed in the waist or more precisely he appears to have stabbed himself because no one was in the washroom at that time and it was locked from the inside. The curator discovered his body. *(he points at an old man standing at one end of the room)*

(They enter the bathroom where the dead body was lying naked on the floor)

159

Sherlock: (*kneeling and examining the body*) He has been stabbed very cleanly….. Lestrade, have you any ideas?

Lestrade: Till now, none.

Sherlock: Hm, of course. (*stands up, and beats his head three times*) Lestrade, Ah….could you please bring me his clothes?

John: His clothes?? For what purpose?

Sherlock: Just do as I say.

Lestrade: (*nods his head*) Bring me the suspect's clothes!!

(*A police officer brings the security boy's clothes and hands them to Lestrade and Sherlock takes them from him and searches impatiently*)

John: What are you looking for?

Sherlock: This! (*he holds a part of the uniform that's been cut*) He's been stabbed with clothes on. If it were a suicide he could not have opened them after he stabbed himself, so clearly he's been murdered.

Lestrade: But why would the murderer open his clothes??? And if there was someone else here where would he go? There's no way out. Did he just vanish?

Sherlock: (*looks down towards the body*) John call your clinic and say you will not be able to make it in today. Oh! it's gonna be interesting. (*then he walks away*)

John: Wait….what? What makes you think I have time to spare for you? But I have my own work. Is this any business of yours?

Sherlock: John, this is of course my business. Now don't be the drama queen and come with me. (*Sherlock exits and John follows him*)

SCENE 3: National Museum Control Room. Sherlock and John enter the scene and approach a man sitting in front of the computer scene.

Sherlock: So you have nothing? Did anyone else enter the washroom at that time?

CCTV operator: No I have checked it a lot of times but no one was in the washroom then nor did anyone enter after that.

Sherlock: Okay, play me the footage of the entrance at the time of the murder. (*he nods and turns on the footage. Sherlock takes a look at the screen and examines everybody who's come in. Suddenly, Lestrade comes running in the rooms and leans against a wall sweating*)

Lestrade: There's been another one, guys. (*he shows a photo of a nude dead man lying on his bed*) It's same method, murder by stabbing in the waist. The only difference is that he was murdered in his the bedroom of his flat.. All the doors and windows were locked from the inside. I have already checked, his clothes were pierced too It is the 23rd floor, the murdered could not have jumped to make his escape. So what do you think now Sherlock?

Sherlock: (*thinks for a second*) Is there any connection between the two men?

Lestrade: I have no idea yet.

John: Any criminal records?

Lestrade: That's the information I have been waiting for.(*his mobile pings*)Yes, he has got a record. Last year he was convicted of smuggling. I handled his case. The thing was recovered later from him.

Sherlock: Thing? What thing?

Lestrade: "The Imperial Faberge Eggs"

Sherlock: (*Sherlock's expression changes, he's shocked. Then he looks away towards the computer screen and suddenly screams*) STOP! (*the operator understands, and pauses the footage*) ZOOM IN! (*he zooms in on the frame and a photo of a blonde woman appears on the screen*)

John: Jesus Christ! That can't impossible!

Lestrade: What is it? What's so special about this woman?

John: Sherlock, I don't understand. That woman was supposed to be dead forty years ago!

Sherlock: Just shut up! (*he closes his eyes and thinks to himself*) the woman, how can she be alive...two men murdered- one security guard and one smuggler ...... the artefact..... what if the murderer is after it....... (*then he asks Lestrade*) Give me your phone quickly(*Lestrade takes out his phone and hands it to Sherlock*)

John: What are you searching for?

Sherlock: (*points the phone screen towards John*) The artefact was handed to the National Museum after recovery. *(then he again closes his eyes and talks to himself*)...to possess something or better steal... first you remove the security.... Then the person who had it or smuggled it... and then you remove the person who currently possesses it.... (*he opens his eyes and walks to the CCTV operator*) Are there any artefacts that are not kept on display?

CCTV operator: Only the ones that are not yet approved by the government. The curator keeps them.

Sherlock: Oh no! Where is the curator?

Lestrade: He went to his room. He said he was feeling sick.

Sherlock: Run, quick! He's going to get murdered. (*The three of the dash away*)

SCENE 3: The three men enter a corridor running. Then they knock on a door.

Lestrade: Mr. Sauniere, please open the door!

John: Open the DOOR!

Sherlock: Open the door, we believe your life is in danger.

Sauniere: (*laughs*) It always is, if you have to look after such priceless artefacts your life will always be in danger.

Sherlock: Don't be a fool, whoever is after your life can get in there and kill you, just like your security guard. We can help you.

Sauniere: Ah! The Invisible Murderer! You cannot save me. If you can, solve the case then.

John: Open the door, it is not the time for games.(*Sherlock steps back from the door*)

Sauniere: Mr. Lestrade, ask your friend how were the two people murdered, only then will I open the door.

Lestrade: (*to Sherlock*) Solve it (*Sherlock gives him a confused look*) Solve the case.

Sherlock: I could not a few minutes ago, what makes you think I can now?

Lestrade: Because now it's necessary. A man's life is at stake. Solve the damn thing!

Sherlock: I don't know, um…..

John: Hold it there. You are not a puzzle solver, you never were, you are just a precocious Drama Queen. You wanted an interesting case, now here's a case, The game is on. Solve it.

Sherlock: (*Unconsciously nods, then he close his eyes and place his index fingers on each side of his head and again starts to talk to himself*) The woman.... how can that happen.... kick the woman out of your mind... two people already murdered... by the same person....for getting some priceless artefact... the murderer vanished out of the room. Well that's clearly not what happened, it's something else.....two people murdered in locked rooms.....both were found naked.... Why did the murderer open their clothes..... but there was... no one in there...they must have opened their clothes themselves....but they were stabbed with clothes on.....so they died after they removed the clothes..........(*then he opens his eyes and turns to Lestrade*) The smuggler.....ah...was he wearing..... a belt?

Lestrade: Yes he was.

Sherlock: (*knocks the door*) I have solved the case, now open the door.

Sauniere: Tell me, how will he kill me?

Sherlock: I believe the process of your murder started several hours ago.

John: What!?

Sherlock: You have been stabbed several hours ago, your belt is what is keeping you alive. (*then he turns to Lestrade*) the murderer used some long pointed nail, applied some poison on it and cleanly stabbed them in their belt... now the tight belts hold the body together and doesn't allow the poison to flow but the moment you open the belt, you die. (*Lestrade and John nod their heads*)

Sauniere: Then I believe I am long dead. Thanks for what you did for me. I shall die in peace.

John: No wait we can help you. We can surely do something.

Sherlock: Don't worry we've already called for the paramedics. You come out, we made a deal.

Lestrade: Step aside guys, I think I will need to break open the door.

(*Lestrade prepares to break the door but the door opens itself and Sauniere comes out*)

Scene 4: 221b sitting-room later that evening Sherlock sits on one sofa when John enters the room.

John: Busy day, wasn't it?

Sherlock: You could say that.

John: I just did.

Sherlock: Funny man!

John: I am happy that the curator was saved.

Sherlock: And the The Imperial Faberge Eggs too.

John: One thing I couldn't understand. Who was that woman?

Sherlock: Only one thing, John? Ah! You have come to the crux of the matter. So, what do you think- who was it?

John: Umm…the daughter of the woman who was in the photograph?

Sherlock: What?! It's never the mothers or daughters. This is not fiction!

John: You mean you believe it's a ghost?!

Sherlock: Don't be absurd. (*suddenly there is a knock on the door*) Why don't you find out yourself? (*Johns goes and opens the door- The CCTV operator and a blonde woman enter the room*)

John: (*shocked looking at the woman*)You?!... (*turns to Sherlock*) Sherlock, what is she doing here? Who is she?

Sherlock: I invited her. (*He stands up*) Come and sit. (the two of them sit down) John, may I introduce you to Mr. and Mrs. Eaton.

John: (*still surprised, looks at the CCTV operator*) This is your wife?

CCTV operator: Yeah, I was surprised when you acted like that seeing her in the footage

John: I don't understand anything. Sherlock would you please explain to me what's happening?

Sherlock: Sure, first to start with her, she's the same woman from the photo and Mr. Eaton who is better known to us as Mr. Dean Whittaker or the Invisible murderer.....

CCTV operator: I don't understand. What do you mean?

Sherlock: Oh, come now. Who is the only person who always stays inside a building but does not appear on the screen- the CCTV operator. First you sent me the that email to distract me... then you stabbed the three of them... you yourself asked your wife to come to the museum and also to pick up the uniforms from laundry. All these would clearly make your wife appear as the criminal but you made a mistake. You faked the image and sent it to me but there was a problem with it. (*he brings the photograph out of his pocket and points to an army officer*) The symbol of arrow in his uniform was launched just last year then how can the photo have been taken forty years ago? (*suddenly*

Lestrade bursts dramatically into the room, Sherlock looks almost admiringly at Lestrade) Inspector, just in time, you will need to make an arrest. (*the woman starts crying . Eaton tries to run but is intercepted by Lestrade*)

Eaton: I should have just killed him. I should not have tried to be too damn clever.(*Lestrade takes him away*)

Sherlock: Don't cry, he was never your husband was he? It was just a sham. (*the woman still cries*) I am sorry, I am really sorry. John, help me! (*John pats Sherlock's back*)

John: There, there, Sherlock.

Soham Bagchi's Top Ten:

1. A Study in Scarlet
2. A Scandal in Bohemia
3. The Man with the Twisted Lip
4. The Adventure of the Musgrave Ritual
5. The Adventure of the Final Problem
6. The Hound of the Baskervilles
7. The Adventure of the Empty House
8. The Adventure of the Dying Detective
9. A Case of Identity
10. The Adventure of the Devil's Foot

Sherlock Holmes vs MasterChef...David Ruffle

The day I took up residence at 221b Baker Street together with Mr Sherlock Holmes has long remained in my memory. Every minute of that day remains crystal clear to me when all too often these days I find I can barely remember what I did yesterday. It was a day that even at a very early stage in our friendship served to illustrate just how single-minded my new friend was. Hardly had he finished telling where I would be sleeping, where my possessions should go and where my chair would reside in the sitting-room when he told me of a test he proposed to foist upon Mrs Hudson who was our landlady.

After a period of unpacking he called that good lady to our sitting-room and outlined this test to her.

'What I want you to do, Mrs Hudson, is to prepare a three course meal for the good doctor and me. This can be a meal of your own choosing, with ingredients of your choice. This will be your chance to impress us, to amaze us with your signature dish.'

'My what?' spluttered Mrs Hudson. 'I have never heard such nonsense. None of my previous tenants have had any complaints about the fare I have produced for them.'

'Perhaps their standards were less exacting than my own.' Holmes consulted his watch. 'It is four o' clock now, shall we say six o'clock? That gives you two hours, Mrs Hudson. Let's cook.'

Holmes ushered a protesting Mrs Hudson out of the room and away down the stairs. I thought his manner most brusque, condescending and patronising and in spite of our friendship being so new I wasted no time in telling him so.

'We are paying tenants here and as such, Mrs Hudson is our landlady not our servant.'

169

'Exactly so, Watson. Is it not then logical that we find out from the onset just what we get for our shillings? If the food is not up to a certain standard then we may find we have to dine out a great deal.'

'I fear dining out may be beyond the funds provided by my pension, Holmes.'

'I do apologise for my thoughtlessness. I meant of course that *I* would have to dine out.'

After a loud and prolonged harrumphing from me, which I hoped he would take as a further criticism we adjourned to the kitchen to check on Mrs Hudson's progress. As befits Victorian gentlemen we were totally unfamiliar with kitchens in general. I for instance had not seen the inside of a kitchen since I was fifteen when our friendly cook or one of her even friendlier girls would give me occasional treats; of course that had nothing to do with (*Editor's note: Here the manuscript is faded and rather illegible. Rather than making wild and speculative guesses as to Watson's words I have decided to leave a blank. The reader is of course free to indulge in such guesses as they see fit*).

'What are you creating for us, Mrs Hudson?' asked Holmes.

'Cooking is what I am doing, not creating. It will be kippers to start on a bed of lightly tossed lettuce. Then braised pork with fried apples and a red wine reduction plus a medley of winter vegetables roasted with bone marrow.'

'Bone marrow?' I queried. 'I have never heard of anyone cooking with that before. Are you sure, Mrs Hudson?'

'Are you in my kitchen or nae?'

'Well, yours of course.'

'Then allow me to continue. The sweet will be bread and butter pudding with a caramel sauce and sugar strand topping.'

'I fear you have left yourself a lot to do, my dear lady. Are you confident you have the time to create this ambitious dish?' Holmes asked.

'If I fail I will be like the fish I had yesterday."

'How do you mean,' I asked.

'Gutted,' she replied.

'Good luck, Mrs Hudson,' said Holmes. 'Dr Watson, at various intervals, will bellow out in a strident manner how much cooking time you have left.

"Gutted," I thought. What a quaint expression and made a mental note never to use it in polite company. When we were once more ensconced in the sitting-room Holmes asked for my views on the menu Mrs Hudson was favouring us with.

'Well, I have to say that she may have bitten off more than she or possibly we can chew. There seems to be a tremendous amount of preparation to get through before she can even thinking of cooking the food itself.'

'I agree, Watson and even though the food is fairly simple fare it is no easy matter to make those individual elements work together. Fish followed by the richness of pork and then the sticky sweetness of that pudding. Cooking doesn't get any tougher than this. I really hope she can pull this off and bring the whole thing together. If she fails, then she will be heading home.'

'But, she is home.'

'Oh, yes so she is.'

'I am really looking forward to the bread and butter pudding. I am very much a pudding person.'

'Your shape rather gives credence to that statement, Watson. Well, we will possess our souls in patience for now.'

When an hour had gone by I was dispatched by Holmes to announce to Mrs Hudson that she had an hour of cooking time left. This I did in an *overly* strident manner causing a startled Mrs Hudson to drop a large casserole dish onto the floor. During the negotiations that followed I made the concession to sell my bull-pup to cover the cost of replacing said dish.

When I was once again dispatched by Holmes on the thirty minute mark I took the not unreasonable view that discretion is the better part of valour and elected to simply shout down the stairs. Some words of Mrs Hudson wafted back up to me, 'stupid sausage neck' or something akin to that. Odd, I could not recall sausage being on the menu. It was just a few minutes past six when Mrs Hudson set down three plates of food before us.

'First of all, Mrs Hudson,' Holmes said, 'the dishes are nicely presented. Nevertheless, there are issues here. The kippers are off-centre giving the plate an untidy look, don't you agree, Doctor?'

'The contents interest me much more than the appearance, can't we just eat the blessed meal?'

'Very well, Watson. Holmes lifted a forkful to his mouth. 'The kippers are cooked to perfection. I commend you. The pork could certainly be improved by a touch more seasoning, but the overall effect is pleasing I must say. You have stepped up to the plate.'

'What?' asked Mrs Hudson.

'What?' I asked.

'You are not familiar with the expression? Oh well, it is of no matter.'

'Mmm…that bread and butter pudding with that caramel is sweet, sticky heaven, Holmes.'

'I will have to take your word for that as you appear to have eaten every last crumb of it. Mrs Hudson, you have done very well. The balance of flavours was just right and you quite obviously know what you are doing in the kitchen. You may therefore cook for us on a daily basis,' Holmes announced, ushering her towards the door.

Mrs Hudson, having been dismissed thus, walked to the door, shaking her head. As she opened it she looked back at Holmes, who was now engrossed in looking out of the window. She raised her middle finger in an extraordinary upward motion and left the room. I was not altogether sure what this gesture meant, but I resolved never to ask her.

'What is it, Holmes?'
'It's an unstable table, Watson.

The Adventure of the Unfathomable Silence...Craig Janacek

The bugle has sounded its last post. The pens have been laid down in the railway carriage at Compiègne. The eleventh hour of the eleventh day of the eleventh month has finally signalled the end of the Great War and its unspeakable horrors. Far too many loved ones forever sleep beneath the poppies and the singing larks. But now that the Prussian yoke has been thrown off, and peace reigns upon the fields of Flanders, I can finally set down one of the stories of how my friend, Mr. Sherlock Holmes, did his part to try to stave off the madness which eventually engulfed both Europe and the world at large. In so doing, I believe that he delayed the onset of that terrible event by some five years, until the efforts of one man – no matter how brilliant – proved to be insufficient to prevent the unyielding beast from finally throwing off its shackles and catching us all up in its gaping maw.

Between the time that Holmes retired from his career as the world's first and foremost consulting detective and the onset of the War to End All Wars, my journal entries had grown far less frequent and interesting. Hence, the events of June, 1909 stand out like a supernova against the dark sky.

It began with what seemed like a simple mistake. My wife and I had travelled up from Southsea in order to take in a show at the Haymarket Theatre. Afterwards, we were dining at Simpsons, when the waiter left two slips of paper upon the table. One was clearly the bill; however, I figured the second must belong to another table. I waved the man over.

"Is there a problem, sir?" he asked.

"I think you have left one slip too many, my good man," said I.

"Have I, sir?" he replied, his voice even. "Are you certain?"

Frowning, I glanced down at the papers. One was a standard cheque; the other was something far different. It was a typewritten note, printed upon the same sort of paper as the Simpsons bill. I read:

Please send your wife back to Claridges and do me the honour of joining me at No. 10, Pall Mall.
– M.

There could only be one man who would send a cryptic note in such a peculiar fashion. But what did Mycroft Holmes want of me, I wondered?

Given the quietude of my current situation, my curiosity was stoked, which made it certain that I would obey his commands. I settled my wife in a hansom cab, and took the opportunity to walk the short distance over to the Diogenes Club. The great warp-and-weft of London passed by, and for a moment, I could without difficulty imagine that I was on some errand commanded by Holmes, the dénouement of a case hanging in the balance. Once a man has lived a life filled with the most thrilling adventures, it can be a difficult thing to adjust to less-rousing circumstances.

I stopped at the familiar door, which was located some little distance from the Carlton. The door was unusual for its lack of a knocker, as the Club employed a footman to be on the constant lookout for expected visitors – all others being not welcome. The door swung open silently, and I made my way down the hall past the window overlooking the sitting room, with its plethora of little nooks. A set of double doors led into the small chamber with the sobriquet of the Stranger's Room, the only locale within the building where the sounds of the human voice were permitted. I was assured that this room possessed the thickest walls of any building in London, save only those belonging to the Old Lady of Threadneedle Street. Its bow-window gazed out over the street, which was deserted at this late hour.

Mycroft Holmes had little changed since I last encountered him. My friend might have been able to determine if his brother had added a few additional pounds to his already considerable girth, but my eyes were not up to the task. In all other aspects, he seemed remarkably like my friend, with that sharp expression in his peculiar deep-set, steel-grey eyes.

"Good evening, Doctor. A pleasure to see you again," said he, leaning forward slightly in order to shake my hand. "It's been since the resolution of the Buckland Abbey case, if I recall?"

"Likewise, Mr. Holmes. Your memory is, of course, accurate. However, I doubt you interrupted my aperitif simply in order to make pleasantries and reminisce about old times?"

He snorted and smiled. "Sherlock always said you had a pawky sense of humour. You are correct, Doctor. I have called you here upon a subject of the greatest importance."

"Unless you have a case of dropsy or of the chilblains, you might have the wrong man. You may perhaps have noted that the Firm has closed up shop? My days as unofficial biographer to Sherlock Holmes are long past."

Mycroft shook his head. "Retirement is not the end, Dr. Watson. Merely the beginning of a new chapter. And when the British Government requires your assistance, it is no small matter to turn it down."

"I wouldn't dream of it. However, I think you must take a trip down to Fulworth. If there are serious events afoot, you should speak to your brother."

"I have tried. But he will not listen. He has always had a curious stubborn streak. You are one of the few men – perhaps the only man – to whom he will, upon occasion, listen. That is why I need you to make one of your occasional week-end visits. You must incite him into looking into this problem. It won't even take him far from his magnificent Channel view. In two hours, the Southern rail will have you both in Portsmouth Harbour. No need for Sherlock to breathe the dense yellow fogs of London again."

I shrugged. "I am happy to try, of course, though I doubt that he will be any more amendable to my pleadings. He has resisted all previous attempts to pry him from Sussex."

"This is no trivial conundrum of the police court, Doctor. He might feel different if he awakens one morning only to find the southern slope of the Downs crawling with Prussians."

My eyebrows rose in alarm. "Do you mean war?"

He nodded gravely. "It is a distinct possibility, I fear. The very balance of European relations may hang upon this issue."

"Then pray tell me the details at once! I will not rest until Holmes has solved your problem."

Mycroft smiled. "I knew I could rely upon you, Doctor. Do you recall the little trouble of Cadogan West?"

"Of course," said I, thinking back to that case from a dozen or so years earlier. "Does this involve the plans for the Bruce-Partington submarine again?"

"Not the plans, Doctor. The actual submarine."

"It has been constructed?"

"Indeed. After sufficient funds were quietly snuck through the Estimates, a modified version – based on the re-designs of Mr. Holland – was built."

"So what is the issue?" I asked, slightly confused.

"The prototype submarine has gone missing."

"Missing? Do you mean, lost at sea?"

"Currently, yes."

"Mechanical error?"

"No, we believe not."

I frowned in confusion. "Based upon what?"

"An eye-witness account that suggests something far different," said Mycroft.

"Such as?"

"Well, Doctor, if you believe the report which has so riled the feathers of the Admiralty chaps, a great sea serpent is responsible for the loss of our state-of-the-art submarine."

"A Kraken," said I, as evenly as I could.

"Indeed."

"But you do not agree with the reports?"

177

His brows furrowed. "You accompanied my brother on some four-hundred cases over seventeen years, Dr. Watson. How many spectral dogs did you encounter? How many genuine vampires? How many ghosts?"

I shrugged. "That may be true, but we should not be so rash as to suppose that we yet know all of the inhabitants of the ocean depths. Surely it is within the bounds of possibility that your witness saw some animal that has never been captured or described?"

"Fictions, Doctor."

"Not according to Aristotle."[1]

"Hearsay."

"Sir Humphrey Gilbert, half-brother of Sir Walter Raleigh, reported encountering a lion-like monster with glaring eyes upon his voyage home from claiming Newfoundland," said I, in response.

"Drink, or more likely madness," he countered. "The man had a disturbed personality."

"And Captain McQuhae of the HMS *Daedalus* who, along with his crew spotted an enormous serpent off St. Helena in 1848? Or Captain Harrington of the *Castilian*, who witnessed a monster of extraordinary length rear its head out of the same waters, not ten years later? I could go on."

Mycroft frowned and his eyes narrowed as he peered at me. "You are extraordinarily well versed in these matters, Doctor."

"I did some looking into the matter after an acquaintance from my club claimed to have seen one. He was standing on the deck of a steamer with his wife, and they were gazing at the ancient Temple of Poseidon on Cape Sounion. Suddenly, they

---

[1] "In Libya, the serpents are very large. Mariners sailing along the coast have told them how they have seen the bones of many oxen which, it was apparent to them, had been devoured by the serpents. And as their ships sailed on, the serpents came to attack them, some of them throwing themselves upon a trireme and capsizing it" (*Historia Animalium*, 4th Century BCE).

were distracted by something swimming parallel to the ship. They saw a curious creature, with a long neck and large flippers. His belief is that it was a young plesiosaurus."

"I am hardly an expert on these sorts of things, Doctor, however, I am assured that the plesiosaurs went extinct, along with the dinosaurs, millions of years ago, Doctor."

"And yet, I have heard rumours of isolated areas of the Amazon – giant plateaus – where monsters from the dawn of man's existence might still roam, imprisoned and protected by un-scalable cliffs. If possible on land, then certainty the vastness of the ocean – covering more than two thirds of the great globe, and deeper than Mount Everest is tall – could also contain such terrors?"

Mycroft shook his head. "The Royal Navy's official position – and mine – is that there are no abnormally large or dangerous sea monsters."

"Then what happened to your submarine?"

"Either the submarine has been sunk, which would be a great tragedy; or it has been captured, which would be an international incident of the most serious nature. In either case, this would require a precise knowledge of the submarine's location. And there are only two individuals in England with said information. I have had them investigated by my finest men, who have turned up nothing. From what I can gather, they both seem to be the most patriotic of men, with no skeletons in their cupboards. However, one of these men has sold our secret to the Kaiser, and I need to know which, before even more damage is done."

"And where was the submarine based?"

"At the HMS *Dolphin* which – despite its name – is actually a shore establishment located in a blockhouse at Gosport. Do you know it?"

"Across the harbour from Portsmouth, if I recall correctly."

"Very good, Doctor. The fort commands the approach to the harbour, and has stood since the days of the sixth Henry. It is commanded by Commodore Francis Shipton, and his second is Captain Elliott Urquhart. Only they were aware of the submarine's intended course. I have prepared a pair of dossiers on the two men." He indicated a pair of manila envelopes upon the table. "In those, my brother will find everything we know about them."

I picked up the envelopes. "I will ensure that Holmes receives these. Is there anything else I should know?"

"I am sending a C.I.D. man along. You and my brother will need an official voice if you are to arrest a high-ranking member of Her Majesty's Naval Service. I believe that you are familiar with him – an Inspector Hopkins? He shall meet you at Victoria Station tomorrow morning for the seven o'clock train."

Fortunately, my understanding wife thought that a little trip down to Holmes's villa would do me good. Therefore, as the sun began to peek out over the East End the following morning, I set out from Claridges to see my friend again. The youthful figure and alert, eager face of Inspector Stanley Hopkins met me upon the platform at Waterloo station. Hopkins was dressed in a quiet tweed travelling suit, though he retained the erect bearing of one who was accustomed to official uniform.

The trip down to Eastbourne took less than two hours, which Hopkins and I spent reminiscing about the mystery of Woodman's Lee, the killing at Yoxley Old Place, and the perplexing set-back of the Randall gang. After that, I regaled him with the story of how we had located Hatley's sunken Indiaman, the well-deserved death of the brute Giordano, the puzzling disappearance of Drake's Drum, and the horrible deeds of Dr. Everhart.

From Eastbourne, we hired a trap to take us the rest of the way to Fulworth, upon whose edge Holmes's villa was situated. As Hopkins and I approached via the drive, we spotted in the fields behind his house a tall, thin figure, covered in a white one-piece jumpsuit with a veiled safari hat. He was tending to a series of boxes, which I knew from previous visits were the artificial frames for Holmes's beehives. I realised that any attempt to approach the swarms of bees would be foolish in the extreme. Therefore, we waited patiently for Holmes to finish his business. This appeared to have something to do with a small lantern-shaped item which emitted smoke, rather than light. Finally, Holmes extracted something from one of the boxes and replaced the lid.

Moments later, he was striding in our direction. Holmes removed his hat and veil as he walked, and I once more saw the narrow face and hawk-like nose of my friend. His thin lips parted in a smile as he approached. "My dear Watson, and Inspector Hopkins to boot! What a pleasure to have you drop in!"

"Feeding the bees, Mr. Holmes?" the inspector asked.

"No, no! The bees feed themselves, Inspector! Behold the plethora of wildflowers that surround us," said he, waiving his arm about. "The bees miraculous transform them into honey of the highest quality. However, harvesting honey was not my mission today." He held out a chunk of sappy-resin. "Here we have some excellent quality propolis. There is nothing quite like it to seal wood, and the old Stradivarius was looking in sorry need of a new layer of varnish. But come inside; it is time for some coddled eggs. Will you join me, gentlemen? I assure you that Martha prepares the finest in Sussex."

"Holmes, we are here on business…" I began.

"Of course you are, Watson," said Holmes, as he strode off towards the house. "The inspector here is too busy a man for jaunts into the countryside." He turned to my companion. "Still, I must say, Hopkins, that you were a tad slow in wrapping up the Merton Park case. It should have been obvious from the start that it was Chandler. The account in *The Times* – typically garbled and incomplete – was sufficient to tell me that."

Hopkins and I followed him through the French doors and into the breakfast parlour, where a fire had banished the morning's chill from the room.

"You are right, Mr. Holmes," said Hopkins ruefully. "If only I had…"

"Inspector," said I, interrupting. "We are not here to discuss old cases." I faced my friend. "Holmes, I was sent by…"

"My brother. Yes, I know."

"You do? Did he wire you?"

"There was no need." He stopped and smiled for a moment. "Surely my little devices must be evident to you by now, Watson?"

I had little time for games, but I paused to consider things. "Let me guess, Holmes. Some spot of mud upon my pant legs whose distinct colour can only be found upon Pall Mall?"

He threw his head back and laughed. "Nothing so ingenious, I am afraid, my dear Watson. However, you do have two manila envelopes sticking out of your coat pocket with a Whitehall seal. There are relatively few places where a retired former army surgeon and writer could acquire such items. Ah, here we go. Time for some eggs."

Holmes's old ruddy-faced housekeeper, her hair tucked into a country cap, entered the room carrying a large tray filled with Crown Derby china. Martha set down in front of me a white ceramic jar painted with a peach. Although time was of the essence, I lifted off the metal lid and the smell of the eggs wafted over me to the point where I realised that I was famished.

"I suppose it wouldn't hurt to eat while we talk. Thank you, Martha. Now, then, Holmes, the case concerns...."

Holmes held up a hand to forestall me. "Have you forgotten that I am retired, Watson?"

"Mycroft says this is of the utmost importance."

"Yes, yes, as were a baker's dozen other matters which have arisen over the last five years. Mycroft grew overly reliant upon having access to my services when we resided at Baker Street. If he ever bothered to stir from his armchair, he might be able to look into things himself." He shook his head. "However, Mycroft's lack of energy now proves to be his Achilles' heel."

"But this will not require much effort, Holmes. Just a short trip along the coast."

"You know that I keep to a strict schedule, Watson. After tending to the bees, I break my fast, and then spend a solid three hours engaged in the composition of my magnum opus. A light supper is followed by a constitutional walk about the cliffs. And then I devote my time to a consideration of philosophy. I am currently most intrigued by Schopenhauer's *World as Will*. Do you know it, Hopkins?"

"I am afraid that I haven't got to that one yet," stammered the inspector.

"I highly recommend it. He shares certain tenets with some gentlemen with whom I became acquainted while journeying in Tibet."

"I would think, Holmes, that you might be interested in a problem which was so complex that your brother was unable to work out the explanation," said I, testily.

He waved his hand languidly in the direction of the cliffs. "I don't have to go far in order to discover cases of sufficient rarity and abstruseness, Watson."

"Oh yes, I recall you mentioning the singular case of the jellyfish," said I, my voice as even as I could maintain it.

His grey eyes narrowed and he peered at me. "Oh very well, Watson. If you are going to be so pertinacious about the whole thing, then I suppose that it will not hurt to take a quick look into the matter. Stackhurst will survive without our game of chess for one evening. Pray tell, what upheaval has so excited my brother?" He lounged back in his chair and pressed his fingertips together.

I described the case exactly as Mycroft had related it, and handed Holmes the dossiers of the two men with knowledge of the submarine's location.

"Dear me, Watson, this is really rather singular," said Holmes, when my account was complete. "Is this the work of yet another remarkable beast currently unknown to science? If so, we might have another long sea-voyage ahead of us. Don't forget how the *Friesland* affair almost turned out, mind you. However, in the case of a sea-monster, we shan't be needing these." Holmes hefted the envelopes in his hand for a moment, and then casually tossed them upon the fire.

"What are you doing, Holmes?" I exclaimed, as I leapt to my feet and vainly attempting to salvage the papers from the flames.

He shook his head. "You know my methods, Watson. I prefer to begin a case unencumbered by the hypotheses laid out by others. My mind is a *tabula rasa*. Now then, if you will reach over to that bookcase, Inspector, and pull down the Bradshaw's,

183

we should be able to ascertain the time of the next train to Portsmouth.

When our train pulled into the station at Portsmouth Harbour, the first things I noted were a gentle wind blowing off the Solent – carrying with it the crisp briny smell of the sea – and the sun shining brightly off the little whitecaps in the water. We emerged next to the Gun Wharf, where lay the floating hulks that comprised the HMS *Vernon*, the Royal Navy's Torpedo Branch. Upon our right was the Royal Dockyard, from which sailed forth the ships that ruled the waves. From our vantage point, I could just make out the vast chequer-patterned bulk of Nelson's former flagship, the *Victory*, now mouldering away in sad neglect, its days of glory long-forgotten.

We caught a Watermen's steam launch, which ran us across the narrow inlet over to the Gosport peninsula. This stopped at a modest marina across from a church named after St. Ambrose. Hopkins led the way from the quay, along a road which ended at the fort's gate. A guard inspected his credentials, and once satisfied, signalled to another marine. This chap motioned for us to follow, and a few minutes later, we were ushered into a plain two-story dun-coloured building, which housed the commander's office.

This proved to be an austere space, with white-washed walls, the severity broken by only a series of coloured nautical flags stained with ink, a spotted white pelt from some great cat, and a bookcase. Upon the latter, I could see a Nautical Almanac, Brassey's *Naval Annual*, Mahan's *Life of Nelson* and his *Influence of Sea Power*, amongst many others. As we entered, a man looked up from behind the desk. Although he was seated, I could tell that he was a tall man, with a sharp face – lined by years at sea – and curling hair long since passed into grey. His blue eyes were intelligent and piercing.

"Welcome to the HMS *Dolphin*, gentlemen," said he, gravely. "I am Commodore Francis Shipton. I am glad for your assistance in this matter, Mr. Holmes."

"Shipton," said Holmes, his eyes darting about the room. "Any relation to Sir George Edward Shipton, once British Minister to Nepal?"

184

"Indeed. He was my father."

"Ah, I thought so. A good man, your father. If memory serves, he was instrumental in securing the support of the Rana Dynasty during the Indian Rebellion. He even received a Companion of the Bath for his outstanding civil service."

"That is correct, Mr. Holmes. I hope to live up to his memory in my own way by ensuring that we retain control over the seas in any future conflict."

"We will need to ask you a few questions, Commodore Shipton, about the missing submarine," Holmes continued.

"Of course, I am happy to provide you with any information in my power. However, we will want to wait for my executive officer, Captain Elliott Urquhart, to arrive. His testimony may prove critical. Ah, here he comes now," Shipton concluded, nodding towards a man who was striding down the hall outside the office.

Once he had joined our group, Captain Urquhart proved to be a short, rather stout, Scotsman. He had eyes so dark that it was difficult to distinguish the pupils, and his face was heavily pocked. His pate was completely bald, however, a bushy moustache drooped over his lips, between which was continuously clenched an amber pipe.

After all introductions had been made, the five of us gathered about the desk, as if engaged in a convention of war. "Pray start at the beginning, if you please, gentlemen," said Holmes, instinctively taking charge over these grizzled naval commanders now that we were in his element.

"Have you been briefed regarding the Bruce-Partington submarine?" asked Shipton.

Holmes nodded. "Watson and I are well aware of its importance," said he, dryly. "I doubt that Whitehall has provided any details to Inspector Hopkins here, however, you may be assured of his discretion in these matters."

Shipton nodded. "Very good. Then you are aware that its technological advances promise to revolutionize naval warfare. The plans are a carefully guarded secret, however, the actual working submarines are just as important as the schematics.

Should one fall into enemy hands, it would be simplicity itself to reverse-engineer the unique aspects."

"And that is what you fear has happened?" Holmes asked.

"Honestly, Mr. Holmes, we don't understand exactly what has transpired. All we know for certain is that the submarine's captain has failed to signal in at the arranged time."

"I have heard it said, Commodore, that a ship is only as good as its captain."

Shipton shook his head. "Commander White is the best man I have. His competence and loyalty to the Crown are indisputable."

"And where was the submarine at the time of its disappearance?"

"The Wadden Sea."

"But that is off the Netherlands!" I exclaimed. "Can submarines travel so far? I thought that they were limited to coastal waters."

Shipton nodded grimly. "That is one of the Bruce-Partington's advances, Doctor. In any case, as soon as Commander White failed to report in via the wireless, we sent our swiftest boat to investigate. Captain Urquhart personally took charge." He nodded at his executive officer.

The Scotsman took over the narrative. "Aye, there was nothing to be seen at the submarine's last known location. But we spotted a few fishing boats, and these eventually led us to a pair of witnesses to the event, a Dutch fisherman and his son in a little boat they called the *Piet Hein*. It took many questions and a considerable amount of time to make sense of their account, which still seems rather extraordinary." He cleared his throat. "I shall read it for you:

'*During the last rays of twilight, we were hauling in the nets for the night before heading back to Delfzijl. Just then, something monstrous broke the water about a hundred yards off our port side. It breathed forth an odour so foul that it seemed to come from the mouth of hell itself. The beast was longer than our ship and spindle-shaped. It was much larger and more rapid than a*

186

whale. The monster was dark grey in colour. It was silent at first, and then it growled, a noise so loud and terrible that it seemed to emanate from all around. After this roar, the beast spit a tongue of flame into the air. It was so hot, we could feel it even at our great distance. We turned our faces away, and when we turned back, the beast had dived back down into the depths, leaving only a roiling sea in its wake. We shook out our sails and made as rapid passage back to home as the Piet Hein *would allow.' "*

Once Urquhart finished his recitation, Holmes snorted in wry amusement.

"Do you find the loss of our submarine amusing, Mr. Holmes?" said Commodore Shipton, angrily.

"No. However, I find such fairy tales to be pure lunacy."

"And do you have an alternate explanation?"

Holmes pursed his lips and shook his head. "Not at the moment. It would absurd to deny that the case is a rather abstruse and difficult one. Nevertheless, I promise to look into the matter forthwith, in hopes of determining what happened to your submarine. I have only one further question for you, Captain Urquhart."

"Name it."

"What was the weather like on the day that your submarine vanished?"

"The weather?" said the man, erupting with anger. "What the devil does the weather have to do with anything?"

Inspector Hopkins held out his hand in a placating fashion. "I assure you, Captain, that while Mr. Holmes's methods may appear unusual, there is a method to them. Please answer the question."

A wave of emotion rolled over the man's features, but he finally settled down. "Very well. It was rather stormy."

"Clouds all day? No chance of a blue sky?"

The man shook his head. "Not that day."

"Very good. Gentlemen, I hope to have some answers for you shortly."

§

"Now, Watson, do you have any views upon the matter?" asked Holmes, when the three of us had exited the building.

I considered this for a moment. "I would wager on Captain Urquhart being our man."

Holmes raised his heavy dark eyebrows. "Oh? And how did you arrive at a conclusion of his guilt?"

"The story of the sea-monster. You have yourself said – upon many prior occasions – that we must eliminate the impossible. If we are taking as our starting hypothesis that a sea-monster is impossible, then we must ask why was it mentioned at all? There is a deep lake in Scotland that is rumoured to be inhabited by just such a monster – a last remnant of earlier era. Urquhart must have got the idea from that legend."

"But the witness!" protested Inspector Hopkins. "How do you explain that?"

I shook my head. "Bribed, I expect. Do you not agree, Holmes?"

He shook his head. "No, no, Watson. It will not do. It could just as easily as been Commodore Shipton. Did you not notice the pelt and the flags?"

"What of them?"

"First, the pelt belongs to the fabled mountain ghost, the rarely-glimpsed snow leopard. And the flags are not nautical signals, but rather Buddhist prayer flags, inscribed with mantras which promote peace and compassion. Both items are unique to the mountainous valleys of Nepal and Tibet. Commodore Shipton was raised by his Foreign Minister father in that remote land, where he would have heard the legend of the Yeti. The legend of the wild-man of the Himalayas could have just as easily spurred the fantastic idea of a monster from the depths of time. No, I am afraid that we cannot cast aspersions upon such fine men upon the basis of such weak suspicions."

"But your brother said that only these two men knew where the submarine was going to be upon that evening. It must be one of them."

"Not necessarily, Watson. In fact, I can assure you that both of those men are innocent."

"On what basis?"

"On the basis of the dossiers, of course."

"But you didn't even read them!" I protested.

"No. However, my brother did. I have told you before that Mycroft possesses even greater powers of observation and deduction than myself. If Mycroft could find no proof of their guilt, *ergo*, it is impossible for them to be guilty. Therefore, we must consider alternative explanations."

"Surely you do not subscribe to the sea-monster theory?"

He chuckled. "No, I do not."

"So, like your brother, you too doubt their existence? That all of the witnesses whom have reported seeing monsters, in every sea and ocean around the globe, were all drunk, or hallucinating, or lying?"

"Not at all, Watson. Although the great cave-bear of Castleton ultimately proved to be a hoax, not all prehistoric remnants are untrue. Take the oarfish, for example."

I shook my head. "What is an oarfish?"

"It is a most peculiar creature. I first read about it in Wood's *Out of Doors*. It looks like nothing less than a giant serpent, and can grow to great lengths. One that washed ashore upon Bermuda a few decades ago was sixteen feet, however, some have been reported to be as long as fifty. They typically inhabit the depths of the ocean, rarely appearing near the surface."

"And what does this have to do with the missing submarine?"

"Very little, Watson, save that the mind is a peculiar machine. When it sees something wholly unexpected, it attempts to construct an explanation from the bits of other ideas that it has stored away. The Dutch fisherman certainly witnessed something odd out there upon the Wadden Sea and – lacking any other frame of reference – he naturally assumed it must have been one of the mythical sea-serpents whose lore is disseminated by sailors in ports around the world."

"So what was the unexpected thing that he observed?"

189

"That is precisely what I am attempting to determine, Watson. I have generated several hypotheses which would serve, however, at the moment I am missing one critical piece of information."

"Which is?" I asked.

Just then, the bell began to toll in the church behind us. When it had concluded its chimes, I noted a sudden glimmer appear in Holmes' grey eyes. I could tell from our long years of association that an idea had occurred to him.

He turned to our companion from Scotland Yard. "Hopkins, we should split up. Do you see that watering hole?" He pointed to a tavern so close to the water's edge it was practically situated upon the dock itself. "The men gathered there might be a source of information about the workings of this base. Unless security is more far lax than Mycroft's information suggests, the sailors won't know anything about the missing submarine itself, of course. However, you should endeavour to see if they can shed any light upon the matter. Ask them about peculiar men seen in the area, that sort of thing."

"Very well, Mr. Holmes," answered the inspector. "But what are you and Dr. Watson going to do?"

"It is difficult to work upon so delightful a day, when all of Nature is newly washed and fresh. Watson and I are going to take a little stroll along the quays in order to enjoy the exquisite air."

Hopkins briefly appeared surprised by this apparent shirking of Holmes's duty. However, the inspector hid his disappointment well and scurried off to perform the task set out for him by Holmes.

I, on the other hand, knew something was afoot. Holmes never had time for poetry when on a case, and even now that he was officially retired, I sincerely doubted that this proclamation contained any element of truth. Therefore, I watched Hopkins go for a moment, and then turned to my friend. "All right, Holmes, what are you up to?"

He smiled. "It is good to have you by my side again, Watson. The inspector is a good man, though he still has yet to fully employ the rules of criminal investigation. Furthermore, even in his travelling outfit, Hopkins still carries himself with the air of a detective, don't you think?"

"I suppose so."

"I assure you that I am correct, Watson. Hopkins will learn nothing in that tavern, as the men within will instinctively recognize him for what he is, and will close up tighter than an oyster with a pearl. That is why I didn't wish for him to accompany us while we sought wisdom amongst the men upon the fishing boats over yonder. And yet, Hopkins will be close enough to rapidly recall should we spot something of interest

We spent the next hour talking to a dozen or so fisherman about a variety of topics – including the weather, the quality of the season's catch, and the fortunes of the local rugby league – none of which, as far as I could tell, had anything to do with the Navy's missing submarine. However, each boat was rapidly dismissed by Holmes, who then moved on to the next with an ever-darkening expression upon his face.

"Our efforts have thus far been in vain, Watson," said he, grimly. "Let us hope that the next boat proves more interesting."

This turned out to be a small schooner, tied up about three-quarters of the way down one of the jetties. The name *Duke of Normandy* was painted upon its stern. As we approached, three men who had been working upon its deck turned in our direction. Two were enormous young men, both over fifteen stone of solid bone and muscle, who gazed upon us silently with faces that could have been carved from granite. The final member of the trio was an older man, with a shock of white hair protruding from beneath a nautical cap. He was much thinner than his companions, and his face was rather red from exertion and exposure to sun. He wore spectacles over intelligent green eyes, and a pair of field glasses dangled from a strap around his neck.

"I am Mr. Harris, of Bermondsey, and this is Mr. Price, of Birmingham," began Holmes. "We have been seeking a boat for hire."

"For what purpose? We run an honest operation here," answered the older man. I detected a trace of an accent in his voice, though I was unable to place its origin.

Holmes laughed. "Nothing nefarious, I assure you, sir. My friend and I are famous sport fishermen. However, we have grown tired of seeking trout and pike in the streams and lakes of England. We wish to test our mettle against some of the bigger beasts of the open water."

The older man shook his head. "I am afraid that we are simple net fishers, Mr. Harris. The *Duke* does not carry the proper equipment for line sport. I don't believe that we can be of any assistance."

"Ah, I am most sorry to hear that," replied Holmes. "My friend and I have been having the devil of a time finding someone to take us out. Do you have any suggestions for other boats at which to inquire?"

"Unfortunately not, Mr. Harris. Gosport is not our home anchorage, so we don't know the men around here well. We have merely followed the cod over to this side of the Solent."

"Ah, I see," said Holmes, disappointedly. "Very well, then. We will keep asking around." He turned to leave, and then stopped. Holmes spun back around, as another question appeared to have just occurred to him. "And if we were chasing after swordfish, where would you seek them, sir?"

The man shrugged. "Swordfish only occasionally migrate through the Channel, Mr. Harris. But I have seen them near our home isle from time to time. We hail from Guernsey. I suggest you try off its shores once you locate a boat for hire."

"Capital! I thank you for your advice, sir." With that, Holmes turned around and began to walk back in the direction of the shore. He took my arm, and muttered under his breath. "Walk normally, Watson, and don't look back. We must trust that they believe that we have been fooled by their little act."

"Is he our man?"

"Most certainly. Did you not notice, Watson that compared to each of the other boats we inspected, their boat had brought in a rather small catch? It is as if they had other things on their minds while at sea, and the catch was merely a smokescreen. Furthermore, did you perceive his accent?"

192

"Of course, Holmes," I protested. "However, simply because the man hails from Guernsey hardly makes him a suspect."

"That man is no more from the Channel Islands than I am, Watson! Unless I have forgotten everything I once knew, that man's accent is from Frisia."

"Frisia?" I asked, frowning in confusion. "Aren't those islands part of Germany?"

"Precisely, Watson. And most importantly, they lie in the midst of the Wadden Sea."

"Then why are we leaving?"

"Because I can tell by the lack of bulge in your coat pocket that you neglected to bring your service revolver."

"I hardly thought it necessary for a trip to the theatre," I replied, defensively.

He waved off my protest. "And though my rheumatism is calmed by these sea airs, I don't wish to unnecessarily test my baritsu skills against those two hulking gentlemen."

"We need the inspector!" I exclaimed.

"Undoubtedly, however, if we wish to learn what happened to the submarine, we first must board that boat. They will destroy the evidence if they see us coming with a member of Scotland Yard. Did you not notice the older man's rather fine set of field glasses?"

"But how are we going to get on board the boat?" I protested.

"First, by resurrecting Captain Basil. And then, by drowning you."

§

Twenty minutes later, I found myself stumbling out of the tavern and down the pier, looking for all the world like a man who had imbibed about three shots of rum too many. Holmes had even made me exchange my regular suit for a set of rough sailor clothes, which he had purchased off of a man in the tavern. I did not bother to resist, for I knew in moments like this that Holmes could never resist a touch of the dramatic.

Long gone was the languid figure whom Hopkins and I had encountered ambling across the fields of Sussex. As he went about detailing his plans in the tavern's front room, Holmes's eager face wore that expression of intense and high-strung energy which I recognized from so many of our adventures together. It was the difference between a thoroughbred put out to pasture, and one set loose upon the Turf of the Wessex Cup.

As I weaved and wobbled slowly towards the *Duke of Normandy*, I knew that Holmes was at that very moment situated in a small dingy, already rowing in a circuitous fashion around the marina, so as to approach the suspect's boat from the rear. Holmes was dressed in a borrowed long overcoat, with a large cap pulled down close over his eyes. He had even managed to produce a tangled, black false beard from some mysterious pocket of his coat. Even I would have had a hard time equating this salty mariner with the respectably-dressed Mr. Harris who had earlier been making inquiries upon the quays.

I knew Inspector Hopkins was watching my progress from behind a curtained window of the tavern, ready to spring into action should Holmes's plan fail to achieve its desired result. I made my way to within a dozen yards of our adversaries' boat, when I paused at the spot indicated by Holmes and leaned over the water, pretending to have a need to evacuate the contents of my stomach. I then slowly toppled into the water, attempting to make this appear like an accident and not part of Holmes's subtle plan to distract our adversaries.

The next several moments were a blur. The water was far colder than I had hoped and the immersion was a bit of a shock to my aging system. But I soon found my way back up to the surface, where I heard cries of alarm being raised. A pounding of footsteps echoed upon the wooden slats of the pier, and a kisby ring attached to a rope was tossed in my direction. I gratefully held onto it while several sets of arms dragged me out of the water.

I lay motionless upon the quay for a few moments, water dripping from my sopping outfit, hoping that my distraction had bought sufficient time for Holmes to board and search the ship. It seemed that our stratagem was successful, for I soon heard the shrill blast of Hopkins's police whistle, which he had loaned to Holmes.

That was the signal for the inspector and me to rush to Holmes's aid. With the help of some marines commandeered from the HMS *Dolphin*, it was only a matter of minutes before the three men had been secured, the leader with a pair of glittering steel handcuffs, and the others with some stout nautical rope. The three of us then proceeded to march our captives back to Commodore Shipton's office. Holmes carried with him a log-book which he had confiscated from the boat's cabin, while behind us, three marines carried a curious, heavy, round metal drum, of some two feet in diameter and less than a foot in depth. Its purpose was a mystery to me, but it was plainly not a part of the traditional gear of a normal fishing trawler.

As we approached the office, Holmes indicated that the two larger captives should be escorted to the fort's brig. The older, bespectacled man was undoubtedly the brains of the operation. This individual was forcefully seated in front of the Commodore, while Captain Urquhart, Inspector Hopkins, Holmes, and I all gathered around him.

"Now then," began Holmes. "Why don't we begin with your name, sir?"

"I am Victor Edwards, from St. Peter Port. I demand to know the reason for this arrest!" said he, angrily. "Of what crime am I accused?"

Holmes smiled. "I asked for your name, *Mein Herr*, not your *nom de guerre*. Your accent suggests that you have never set foot upon Guernsey. It is plain that you hail from one of the Frisian Islands. Nordeney, or Borkum, if I had to guess."

The man licked his lips. "That is absurd. I am..."

"Your cover story may have been sufficient to fool the fisherman of Gosport, *Mein Herr*, but it will not stand up to any real scrutiny. A simple wire over to Guernsey will suffice to sink your little subterfuge. You can either tell me your name now, or I shall be forced to make one up. Shall we call you '*Rache*?' I have always had a fondness for that word," said Holmes, sardonically.

"Ehrenberg," muttered the man.

"Very good, Herr Ehrenberg. Now, with the help of your log-book, I shall relate to Commodore Shipton and Captain Urquhart precisely what you and your men have been up to. After that, I hope that you will find your cell at Fort Charlotte a comfortable one."[2]

"You have no grounds to hold me! This whole proceeding is outrageous," Ehrenberg protested.

"On the contrary. You are guilty of instigating an act of war."

"Pray explain yourself, Mr. Holmes," interjected Commodore Shipton. "Are you claiming that this man is responsible for the disappearance of our submarine?"

"Indeed. Not directly, of course. However, he is the facilitator of its destruction."

"Destruction!" exclaimed Captain Urquhart, his voice hoarse. "Do you mean that the submarine has been lost? It carried a complement of twenty-five men!"

"I am afraid so, Captain," said Holmes, gravely. "The blood of those men is on Herr Ehrenberg's hands. It was he that tracked the submarine's movements. The recordings in his log-book confirm it."

"In a little fishing boat?" said Commodore Shipton, doubtfully. "That is impossible."

"It may have once been impossible, Commodore, unfortunately, that is no longer the case. The idea came to me like the ringing of a bell. With each technological advance we make in the science of war, a simultaneous counter-advance is made. In this case, we built the Bruce-Partington submarine, capable of long-range scouting of the German military installations in the Frisian Islands, at Wilhelmshaven, and at our

---

[2]Fort Charlotte is an artillery fort in Shetland, Scotland. There are no records that it was ever used as a prison, however, here Holmes appears to be implying that it was used for the detainment of top-secret military prisoners.

former colony of Heligoland.[3] In return, Herr Ehrenberg has constructed a method with which to track our submarines. He utilised that curious drum your men left outside the office, which I have yet to closely examine. However, if you turn it over to the government's scientists, I expect that they will shortly determine that it is capable of creating underwater sounds and then picking up any resulting echoes. Given the paucity of whales or other sea-monsters in the Channel, once away from land, any echoes that his sonorous device receives must be coming from an underwater ship."

Both Commodore Shipton and Captain Urquhart had looks of horror upon their faces. "If that is true, Mr. Holmes, then the silent service has been nullified!" cried Shipton. "There is no further advantage for our submarines."

"I suspect that to be an oversimplification, Commodore. Herr Ehrenberg's device will require some experimentation, and it is likely still a rather crude affair. From an inspection of the boat's logs, it took Ehrenberg and his men several weeks in order to track your submarine. And now that we are in possession of Ehrenberg's device, the Royal Navy will be able to create more. We can employ it against any German submarines sailing from Kiel. The wheel turns, gentlemen."[4]

Shipton shook his head as he mentally digested this information. "There is a major difference, Mr. Holmes, between tracking a submarine and sinking it. How do you propose that transpired?"

---

[3] Heligoland is a small archipelago in the North Sea which came under British control at the end of the Napoleonic Wars. It was traded to Germany in 1890 in exchange for the protectorate over the Zanzibar archipelago.

[4] Ehrenberg's device sounds very similar to a Fessenden oscillator, the first successful acoustical echo ranging device, and a precursor to sonar. Although invented by the Canadian Reginald Fessenden (1866-1932), the German physicist Alexander Behm (1880-1952) obtained a patent for an echo sounder in 1913, so we know Germany was also working on such a device at this time. British H-class submarines, first launched in 1915, were equipped with Fessenden oscillators.

"A torpedo!" I exclaimed. "Ehrenberg may have wired to a destroyer, which then fired the fatal shot."

"Capital, Watson," said Holmes. "However, you are forgetting the account of the witness. Surely the fisherman would not have been so obtuse as to miss the presence of a German destroyer within torpedo's range?"

"But his account is impossible!" I protested.

"Not impossible, merely improbable. I submit that the so-called monster witnessed by our Dutch fisherman was nothing other than the submarine itself. It surfaced in order to send its nightly wireless report, not realising that a small boat might be nearby. It also vented its black-water waste, which produced the foul smell that the man reported."

"And the loud noise?" queried Shipton. "Our submarine makes no such sound."

"Indeed not," said Holmes. "That would have come from the agent of its destruction. The engine of an aeroplane."

"Surely you jest, Mr. Holmes," objected Shipton. "Those lighter-than-air craft can barely fly a hundred yards. Maybe one of Zeppelin's airships?"

"Too slow," Holmes concluded. "No, it can only have been a new model of an aeroplane, capable of a long flight over water. And from that craft, the pilot dropped an explosive charge which blew open a sufficient hole to result in the sinking of your submarine. That was the tongue of fire witnessed by the fisherman."

"You horrify me, Holmes," said I, quietly. "If this is true, then soon Britain may no longer be an island."[5]

---

[5]The first known heavier-than-air aeroplane to cross the English Channel was the Blériot XI in July 1909. Another early aircraft was the Voison II plane bought by Armand Zipfel and flown in Berlin in January 1909. The Farman III, which began to be manufactured in Germany in December 1909 under the name Albatros F-2 flew the first known military mission in Europe in October 1912. However, the earliest recorded use of explosive ordnance dropped from an aircraft occurred in

We all sat quietly for a moment and pondered the implications of this terrible news.

"This is an outrage!" thundered Captain Urquhart, finally breaking the silence. "It is worse than the Dogger Bank incident, for rather than simple incompetence, it was perpetrated as a deliberate act of war."[6]

"That is a question for men who occupy higher seats than I, Captain," said Holmes, calmly. "Herr Ehrenberg's superiors may believe that the Royal Navy was in the wrong for running a submarine so near their own bases. In any case, I think that Inspector Hopkins will see to it that Herr Ehrenberg does not glimpse the light of day again for many years to come, until the brewing storm has cleared." Holmes paused and nodded at the men in the room before turning to me. "And now that this little business has been taken care of, Watson, I think a little stroll is in order. I have a sudden yearning to stride the boards of Nelson's *Victory*."

§

As a word of epilogue, several days later I was comfortably ensconced in my arm-chair at my little Southsea villa reading the local morning paper, when I came across a small article buried at the bottom of page five. It concerned the fishing boat *Duke of Normandy*, of St. Peter Port, Guernsey, which was tragically lost with all hands during an unexpected squall off Bembridge. I was little surprised to find that Mycroft was as equally adept as his brother at utilizing the institution of the press. Therein Mycroft could spread the supposed facts of the

---

November, 1911, when the Italian pilot Giulio Gavotti dropped several grapefruit-sized grenades upon Ottoman positions in Libya.

[7] The Dogger Bank incident occurred in 1904, when the Russian Baltic Fleet mistook a British fleet of fishing trawlers for an advance force of the Imperial Japanese Navy (with whom the Russians were at war). The Russian ships fired upon the British fishermen, killed three and wounding many others.

false narrative that he was crafting for those foreign agents inquiring as to the sudden disappearance of Herr Ehrenberg and his sonorous device.

Sadly, there was no mention in that paper, or any other, of Commander White or his twenty-five men, lost in the unfathomable deep. However, I have it upon good authority that their families were quietly presented with posthumous Conspicuous Service Crosses for their gallantry against the enemy at sea – despite the fact that we currently faced no enemy. There was only that terrible sword of Damocles hanging ominously over our heads from the East. At the moment, the only war was the secret one.... of misinformation and the shield of lies.

Craig Janacek's Top Ten

1. The Hound of the Baskervilles
2. The Sign of Four
3. The Adventure of the Musgrave Ritual
4. The Adventure of the Blue Carbuncle
5. A Study in Scarlet
6. The Valley of Fear
7. The Adventure of the Speckled Band
8. The Adventure of the Six Napoleons
9. The Adventure of the Sussex Vampire
10. Silver Blaze

Retirement...David Ruffle

He may have retired to keep bees

With no more villains to seize

No more stench of London's sleaze

Instead, the delight of the Downs' gentle breeze

Living in Sussex like an outcast

But can a man ever escape his past?

Yes, he may feel so alive

As he tends to his beehive

But does he not know?

Can he not surmise?

For him and for us...it's always 1895.

'What is it, Watson?'

'It's Tales from the Stranger's Room Volume Three, Holmes.'

Those answers......

Sorting out the Suspects

1. Irene Adler **2.** Jack Woodley **3.** (Professor) James Moriarty **4.** (Baron) Adelbert Gruner **5.** Mary Morstan **6.** Violet Hunter **7.** (Doctor) Percy Trevelyan **8.** Helen Stoner **9.** Victor Hatherley **10.** Nathan Garrideb

The Guilty Man

Pietro Venucci is the guilty man. If John Clay or Henry Peters had committed the crime, all of the four given statements would be untrue. If Colonel Moran had been the murderer, three of the four statements would be true (rather than untrue).

Criminal Links

Lauriston from Chapter 3, 'The Lauriston Gardens Mystery', in *A Study in Scarlet*:

I	R	L	S	O	A	N	U	T
A	U	T	L	N	I	O	S	R
O	S	N	U	R	T	I	A	L
L	**A**	**U**	**R**	**I**	**S**	**T**	**O**	**N**
N	I	R	T	U	O	A	L	S
T	O	S	N	A	L	R	I	U
R	L	O	A	S	N	U	T	I
S	N	A	I	T	U	L	R	O
U	T	I	O	L	R	S	N	A

1. Poetic (In)Justice

Verse 1 – killer is the **Soldier** (anagram of 'red soil').

Verse 2 – killer is **Heather** ('Mainly found on open moor' = Heath, added to 'er' from 'Partly in error').

Verse 3 – killed is **Theodore** (anagram of 'other ode').

Verse 4 – killer is **Andrew** (found in the words 'man drew').

Verse 5 – killer is **Freda** (found in the words 'of red ash').

My thanks to all the contributors for donating their work and allowing me to tamper with them (the pieces not the contributors!). Look out for Volume Four at some point in the future. Thanks for dropping by the Stranger's Room.

David Ruffle

Also from MX Publishing

MX Publishing is the world's largest specialist Sherlock Holmes publisher, with over a hundred titles and fifty authors creating the latest in Sherlock Holmes fiction and non-fiction.

From traditional short stories and novels to travel guides and quiz books, MX Publishing cater for all Holmes fans.

The collection includes leading titles such as _Benedict Cumberbatch In Transition_ and _The Norwood Author_ which won the 2011 Howlett Award (Sherlock Holmes Book of the Year).

MX Publishing also has one of the largest communities of Holmes fans on Facebook with regular contributions from dozens of authors.

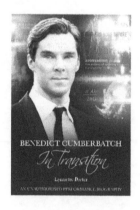

www.mxpublishing.com

Also from MX Publishing

"Phil Growick's, 'The Secret Journal of Dr Watson', is an adventure which takes place in the latter part of Holmes and Watson's lives. They are entrusted by HM Government (although not officially) and the King no less to undertake a rescue mission to save the Romanovs, Russia's Royal family from a grisly end at the hand of the Bolsheviks. There is a wealth of detail in the story but not so much as would detract us from the enjoyment of the story. Espionage, counter-espionage, the ace of spies himself, double-agents, double-crossers...all these flit across the pages in a realistic and exciting way. All the characters are extremely well-drawn and Mr Growick, most importantly, does not falter with a very good ear for Holmesian dialogue indeed. Highly recommended. A five-star effort."
The Baker Street Society

www.mxpublishing.com

Also from MX Publishing

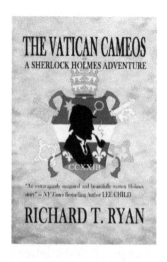

When the papal apartments are burgled in 1901, Sherlock Holmes is summoned to Rome by Pope Leo XII. After learning from the pontiff that several priceless cameos that could prove compromising to the church, and perhaps determine the future of the newly unified Italy, have been stolen, Holmes is asked to recover them. In a parallel story, Michelangelo, the toast of Rome in 1501 after the unveiling of his Pieta, is commissioned by Pope Alexander VI, the last of the Borgia pontiffs, with creating the cameos that will bedevil Holmes and the papacy four centuries later. For fans of Conan Doyle's immortal detective, the game is always afoot. However, the great detective has never encountered an adversary quite like the one with whom he crosses swords in "The Vatican Cameos.."

"An extravagantly imagined and beautifully written Holmes story"
(Lee Child, NY Times Bestselling author, Jack Reacher series)

Lightning Source UK Ltd.
Milton Keynes UK
UKHW021117010520
362588UK00013B/3591